Other books by Judy and Ronald Culp:

The Search for Truth

THE SEA

FOR FREI

THE SEARCH FOR FREEDOM

•

Judy and Ronald Culp

AVALON BOOKS
NEW YORK

Published by Thomas Bouregy & Co., Inc.
160 Madison Avenue, New York, NY 10016

Library of Congress Cataloging-in-Publication Data

Culp, Judy.
    The Search for freedom / Judy and Ronald Culp.
        p.   cm.
    ISBN-13: 978-0-8034-9821-1 (acid-free paper)
    ISBN-10: 0-8034-9821-7 (acid-free paper)
    I. Culp, Ronald.   II. Title.

PS3603.U595S427 2007
813'.6—dc22

                                    2006028590

PRINTED IN THE UNITED STATES OF AMERICA
ON ACID-FREE PAPER
BY HADDON CRAFTSMEN, BLOOMSBURG, PENNSYLVANIA

Faith, family, friends: We need all
to make the journey.
Special thanks to B.J. Stone

Chapter One

"**P**oppa. You are hurting my hand. Besides, it's time for me to go." Lomida tugged at Captain John Law's hand. "I won't be gone long." Her small hand slid free as she looked at the large stagecoach. She danced in place as she waited for her father to lift her into the great pumpkin. She imagined herself to be just like Cinderella in the French fairy tale of *The Little Glass Slipper*, her mother's favorite story. Lomida giggled as she thought of the old tale and tried to picture Miss Maddie, her schoolmistress and chaperone for this trip as the godmother. She was pretty enough, but much too young. Who would the king's son be? As for the rat who became the coachman . . .

"Lomida. I asked you if you were ready to get in the coach."

"Yes, sir." Lomida eagerly held her arms up to her father waiting for his assistance.

The San Antonio and San Diego Southern Overland Mail stagecoach, its once glossy red paint faded and weather-beaten, stood loaded in front of the Fort Davis, Texas, post commissary. The horses exhaled white clouds of breath in the cool air while they snorted and pranced with excitement. Ready to travel, the leaders' reins were held by a wrangler as the driver climbed to his seat, waited for his express guard to get up and put his shotgun to the ready, and finally took up the reins.

A rising winter sun dimmed the stars overhead and brightened the eastern sky. Vertical bluffs of darkly weathered rocks called the Sleeping Lion rose two hundred feet high and rimmed the north and west boundaries of the fort. The rim glowed red in the first light of day. The stage road passed through the fort where the commissary, located across the road from the quartermaster storehouse and corral, served as a makeshift station. Since the Army provided armed guards on the stages for protection against Indian and bandit raids and had been doing so for several years, the stage stopped on post and again at the stage station in the small settlement near the Army post. The town, also called Fort Davis, served as the county seat of Jeff Davis County.

A heavily armed four-man guard detail of 10th U.S. Cavalry Negro troopers, known to the Indians as Buffalo Soldiers for their dark skin and curly hair, stood respectfully apart from the small crowd gathered to see the stage off. Two of the soldiers would ride atop the stagecoach, while the remaining two served as mounted escorts riding behind.

Captain John McCandless Law, the fort's adjutant, hugged his twelve-year-old daughter, gave her a kiss on both cheeks, and then lifted her into the coach where Maddie Brown helped her onto a padded leather seat.

"Miss Maddie, do you have any questions before you two get on your way?"

"No, I think we are ready for any emergency."

"Sweetheart, you could at least pretend to be sad at leaving us," Law chided the precocious little girl for her eagerness to be away.

"Oh, Poppa." Lomida laughed happily. This was to be an adventure, even if the reason for the trip was quite serious.

With a flourish, Maddie pulled a handkerchief from Lomida's small knitted purse, and gave it to her. Maddie, trying not to laugh, pretended to pat Lomida on her dainty shoulders as the child made an elaborate show of boo-hooing while laughing blue eyes peered above the delicate hankie.

The girl dabbed at her eyes. "There. I'm sad."

"Mind Miss Maddie"— her father laughed—"and be sure to write to me with all the details of your visit to the doctor in El Paso. Don't run away and join a traveling troupe of actors."

"Oh, Poppa, I won't. Join the actors I mean. And I promised I would write. We won't be gone that long. School break is only for a few weeks and Miss Maddie has to be back to teach. You know that."

"Don't worry, Captain. She'll be fine with me."

A bugle call sounded—life on an Army post was regulated by such calls—and set the post dogs to howling. This call, "Assembly," sounded in the still morning air as the duty bugler took his post on the parade ground, and John Law heard spoken commands as the officer of the day formed the troops for formal guard mount at the nearby guardhouse. The two soldiers who would ride the stage climbed atop the coach, rifle stocks and heavy boots thumping hollowly on the coach.

Law passed up to Maddie a wicker picnic hamper tied with a red ribbon that the wife of the commissary officer had stocked for the trip—"No Army rations for our travelers! Hard tack and greasy bacon are unfit for delicate young ladies." Law slammed the door closed and stepped away, waving to the driver. As the stage lurched into motion, the driver kept his speed down until he cleared the post. Lomida and Maddie waved handkerchiefs and called cheery "Good-byes" from the window.

Dust flew in all directions so they quickly retreated into the coach. Captain Law watched until the stage passed behind an adobe storehouse at the edge of the post. *Our last chance is the city doctor. Maybe he can do something to help Lomida's leg that our Army surgeons can't. It would be a shame if that riding accident crippled her for life.*

"Good morning, sir."

Law turned and found Quartermaster Sergeant Nathaniel Durbin at attention. Law returned the salute, "Morning, Sergeant."

"Mr. Wordsmith's respects. The guard is formed."

"Very well. Let's go observe guard mount."

The stage settled into a smooth pace on the road west. Maddie arranged a lap quilt to keep them warm in the cool of the morning. She was as excited as the young girl. In her late twenties, Maddie Brown had been teaching school at Fort Davis for the last two years. Tall and slim, at mealtimes Maddie could eat everything in sight although she never gained a pound.

She thought her appetite went back to her younger days when she was always hungry and rarely had enough to eat.

Maddie looked forward to all the comforts El Paso offered. It was a huge city in comparison with Fort Davis. Although she'd never been to the city, after living on a rather primitive frontier Army post she felt that it had to be a bit more "civilized."

"Look," she said to Lomida, "the stationmaster gave me a list of our stops so we'd know where we are."

The girl, already munching on a ham biscuit quietly pulled from the basket, turned from the window. "Show me."

"Do you never get enough to eat? Give me a biscuit as well and I'll share." Maddie laughed. "Here we go," she said, reading from a paper. "It's ten miles to Point of Rocks, and from there nine miles to the Barree Springs station and another thirteen miles to—that's unlucky, isn't it? Thirteen miles to the station at El Muerto where we change horses and stretch."

"El Muerto?" Lomida squealed, "What a horrible name! What does it mean?"

"I'm not sure. But the driver called it Dead Man's Hole." That elicited another squeal from Lomida, thrilled as only a young girl could be with the prospect of her first great adventure in their two-hundred-mile trip across west Texas.

"After our rest, it's thirty-three miles to Van Horn's Wells." Maddie turned to Lomida, simpered and batted her eyes coquettishly. "Maybe we'll see that dashing young Lieutenant Zook, since he has been assigned to the guard detail out there."

"The officer who sang to us when we were promenading last week?"

"And made you blush." Maddie laughed settling back to gaze out the window.

Chapter Two

Joe Bass stepped from the dark interior of the ten-by-twelve adobe hut that served as his office at the El Muerto stage station, hitched up his pants, coughed and spat. The silence was broken only by a gusting wind from the north. The hut shared a wall with a similar adobe that backed up to the station corral. Vertical firing-slits were spaced around the walls in case of Indian attack, an infrequent but ever-present danger since the great Comanche war trail into Mexico passed nearby, and Apache raiders sometimes tried to steal horses from the corrals. Bass squinted in the bright sunlight, shaded his eyes with a flattened hand held to his forehead, and looked down the road for the stage from Fort Davis. Schedules on the frontier were flexible, but he expected to see the coach before noon. He looked at his pocket watch—nearly eleven o'clock. He noticed that the horses in the corral were restless, bunching in one corner, milling, shying away as if a panther or a lobo wolf was nearby.

7

Bass called to his assistant in the cookhouse at the second corral. *"Miguel, que pasa? Donde estan los soldados?"* Where are the soldier guards? Bass thought they were a bunch of no-accounts, probably drunk in the bushes again. Cursing with all the fluency of an experienced muleskinner, Bass walked the short distance to the little camp used by the black cavalry soldiers assigned to guard the station. He'd show them. He stepped around the corner of the cookhouse.

"What the . . ."

Bass caught a momentary glimpse of the rear end of a mule running hard, disappearing over a low rise just north of the station, with Miguel astride the animal's back. The station's soldier guards, without hats, shoes, or carbines, ran barely a hundred yards behind the mule, and almost as quickly disappeared from sight over the rise. Stunned, Bass finally found his voice and shouted, "Hey!" but it was too late. He turned back to the station. Before him stood four men, their hard eyes glittering with hatred. Apaches! Involuntarily, Bass stepped backward as his right hand fumbled at his thigh where his pistol should have been. He'd forgotten to buckle on his gun belt!

Chapter Three

The coach bumped and lurched from side to side, jolted by each rock in the road as it rolled down the poorly kept stage road in far West Texas. Used by a few ranchers, soldiers and supply wagons, the road was more a suggestion than a real thing. With the railroad expected to pass through the country in the coming year, the favored road from the county seat went south and west toward the water wells at the base of the Chinati Mountains, where a town was to be built. One day the road would link Fort Davis and west Texas to civilization. Maddie looked out the coach window just as a wind gust raised a puff of dust as the coach wheeled across a dry stretch of road.

"Ugh. This is *not* civilized!" Maddie muttered to herself as she coughed and pulled an already gritty handkerchief from her purse. Maddie removed her hat and shook the dust from it. She attempted to wipe her face but only ended up smearing the brown grit. The desert dust had nearly ruined the silk flowers so that the hat no

9

longer resembled the once-lovely present that Samuel had so lovingly given her so many months ago. No. It was a little over two years ago. When there was a Samuel, she whispered to herself.

"What did you say, Miss Maddie?" A small hand patted her on the wrist and Maddie turned to face Lomida. She was Maddie's ticket out of Fort Davis for the school holiday. Playing chaperone for Lomida had been a gift in disguise for Maddie. Thanksgiving by herself at the post with all the older ladies looking down their noses at the 'single' schoolteacher was not a very pleasant proposition. No, this had come at the perfect time. A couple of days in El Paso, an opportunity to look for a new position in a real town, discreetly of course, were just what she needed.

"Are you comfortable, Lomida?" Maddie asked as the stage jolted once more.

"I think I'd like to rest. My leg does hurt just a little."

Maddie forgot her own problems as she helped the small girl lie down on the seat.

The horses were tiring as the stage reached the edge of a low mesa where the road followed a downhill grade to the station at El Muerto less than a quarter of a mile distant. Maddie caught part of a murmured question from one of the soldiers on top of the coach, something like, ". . . you see the corporal?"

"Heads up, boys," the driver said. "Something ain't right."

Maddie put her arm protectively around Lomida, while looking out across the deserted plain as the coach slowed at the station yard. A sudden sound of a gunshot and a horse screamed while the coach slewed sideways to a shuddering halt. At the same time a spatter of shots rang out, one of the guards fell off the coach, struck the left rear wheel and collapsed in a heap in the road. The driver grunted, and a man cried, "No, please!" in a terrified voice, followed by the sharp crack of two more shots fired close by the coach. From her window Maddie saw that the right lead horse was down, probably dead, and the other horses of the team were shying away from the smell of blood. The opposite door of the stagecoach jerked open to reveal a fierce Apache warrior. The Indian, a Winchester rifle held loosely in his hands, wore Mexican peasant clothing with a black vest, his long hair held under a brightly colored headband, and two belts of cartridges in cloth loops crossed his chest. The man scowled at a frightened Lomida.

"Get away from that door!" shouted Maddie.

"I want my poppa," wailed Lomida, burying her face in Maddie's shoulder.

More shots rang out behind the coach followed by jubilant shouts and whoops. The Indian looked in the direction of the shouts and called out in a language neither Maddie nor Lomida could understand.

One dark face, then two more, peered in at Maddie. From the opposite side of the coach three more Indians came into view, grim and fierce men, whose agitated, hard eyes glittered with the excited light of battle. One of the men, dressed in a breech-clout over white trousers, a short blue Army jacket over a bare chest, his long dark hair hanging loosely under a white straw hat, reached in to push back her bonnet and touch Maddie's silver-blond hair. The frightened young woman drew back from the Indian's touch. Her fear quickened when she recognized the Indian as someone she had seen at the fort. Half Man, yes, that was it. She remembered with a shudder the way his eyes followed her at the post. Joseph Half Man he was called. He came to the post to see his sister, the one they called Indian Annie, who was Captain Law's cook and housekeeper!

Chapter Four

Lieutenant Solomon J. Burney, 'Sol' to his friends, had a good eye for terrain. He kept his ten-man patrol off the skyline to ride along what engineers at West Point taught was the "military crest of a hill," a few yards below the actual crest of a ridge. His chosen trail offered a commanding view of a good ten square miles of open ground yet provided some concealment from an observer. He was determined *not* to make an inexperienced "shave tail" lieutenant's mistakes and lead his men into an ambush on his first solo patrol. Sol believed he was a lucky man because his first assignment after West Point was with the Black Horse Troop of the 10th U.S. Cavalry Regiment on the Texas frontier. True, it was a regiment of colored troops that Congress formed during the Army's reorganization in 1866 after the Civil War. Some back East looked down on the Negroes as second-rate troops, but it was also a field unit, and that meant a chance to command a file of troopers! On the frontier he soon understood that there was nothing second-rate about them. The Negroes had proved themselves in battle as hard-riding and hard-fighting soldiers, feared and respected by Indians.

Sergeant Alfonse Leoni, the senior noncommissioned officer on the patrol, rode alongside the young lieutenant. Leoni was a rather small and intense man with dark eyes and slicked down black hair he parted in the middle. He enjoyed a reputation as an excellent soldier and had been mentioned in dispatches by General Phil Sheridan for bravery under fire at a small but deadly skirmish with Rebel cavalry near Winchester, Virginia, during the Civil War. Leoni was exceptional in the U.S. Cavalry because he was a tee-totaler who never drank liquor, and because he was devoted to Artemisia, his wife of fifteen years. None of his fellow soldiers knew that Leoni, as an idealistic farm boy in his early teens, had fought in several battles alongside the great Italian patriot Garibaldi in 1860 to remove the Bourbon King Ferdinando II and to unite Italy. During the fighting in Sicily the young Leoni discovered he had an aptitude for war. Later, he also discovered he was unable to return to his former quiet life on the farm. In search of military adventure, he immigrated to America in 1864 and joined the Union Army. While Artemisia, whom he met and married a year later in Philadelphia was his passion, soldiering was his life.

The small patrol was near the end of a seven-day scout to familiarize the newly arrived officer with the terrain near the fort. Sol was awed by the varied land he found, and Leoni intended to teach the young officer as much as he could about their surroundings. For several miles around the fort the prairie was covered with grasses and there were many oaks and juniper trees, with cottonwoods and willows lining clear-flowing streams. Volcanic rocks lay all around while the hills revealed thick layers of dark rocks, evidence of extensive upheaval in the distant past. Mitre Peak, so named for its resemblance to a bishop's ceremonial head covering, appeared to be the remnant of a volcano. To the south they had ridden across desert covered mostly by yuccas and agaves, low grasses, and some creosote bushes, called chaparral locally. Prickly pears and Mormon Tea were profuse along their current route while honey mesquite grew along washes and in the wide playas. Leoni had pointed out white-thorn acacia, allthorn and ocotillo in other parts of their ride across the Chihuahuan Desert.

Men and horses were tired, dusty, and, with supplies nearly exhausted, eager for a good meal and the relative comforts of the fort.

"Lieutenant," Leoni said, pointing to the east across the plain, "look out there."

Sol Burney scanned the desert to his front out to distant hills, bleak under the wintry sun. "I see them. Carrion birds circling those rocks, maybe a mile away."

"Let's look at your map, sir," Leoni said. "Where are we and where exactly are those birds?"

Sol halted the patrol, told Leoni to dismount the men for a ten-minute break and pulled a map from his saddlebags. The tired men stood quietly by their mounts, rubbed aching backsides and stretched stiffened knee joints. Sol quickly oriented his map to the patrol's location. "Mount 'em up, Sergeant. Unless I read the map wrong, those buzzards are circling the El Muerto stage station."

The stagecoach, both doors ajar, stood forlorn and empty in the road, one dead horse still in the harness. Baggage had been thrown from the boot, some of it opened, and pieces of clothing tossed to the ground among moccasin tracks. There were no other horses at the station. Sol Burney had never seen what Apaches did to a captive, and the sight of Joe Bass' remains and the bodies of four cavalrymen, stripped of their uniforms and horribly treated, was seared into his mind. Hardened cavalrymen watched as the young officer turned away in revulsion, shoulders heaving as he retched miserably. No man ever really got used to such a gruesome sight.

"You there, keep those birds off. Skirmishers," Leoni commanded, "move out!" and two of his well-drilled soldiers chambered big .45–.55 cartridges in their Springfield carbines, set the weapons at half-cock and held them at the ready as they moved quickly. Their purpose was to warn the patrol if the Indians returned. Fatigue gave way to keen alertness, for each recognized the nearness of danger. Another man chased the buzzards away.

"No other bodies, Sergeant," a trooper reported after he completed a quick look around the stage station. "Whoever did this, they went south towards Mexico. Looks like half dozen or so Indian ponies, unshod, and they were driving a bunch of shod horses with them. I think one of the ponies is carrying double."

"Good report, trooper."

After allowing his officer a moment to recover his composure, Leoni spoke quietly. "Lieutenant, we can't find the station cook. He's probably hiding out there somewhere if he's lucky. That white man is Bass, the stationmaster, and those other bodies must have been escorts for the stage. We always assign one to ride the stage, with two more at the station. I don't know why we found four here."

"Hey, Sergeant!" the trooper yelled from the stage. "Look here!"

Leoni saw the man point to the floor inside the stage cabin where a hand-crocheted burgundy-colored handbag lay opened, a small oval-framed photograph of a woman beside it. Leoni groaned inwardly, for he recognized that the handbag belonged to little Miss Lomida, the post adjutant's daughter.

Sol Burney stood at the opposite door, and on the worn, cracked leather seat before him he saw a woman's hat. "That belongs to the schoolteacher," Sol said to Sergeant Leoni. "She's an attractive woman. I saw her in it when she came to retreat last Friday. Whose handbag is that?"

"Sir," Leoni said as he examined the bag, "we have a problem. We need to get a rider back to the post as quick as we can."

"Why?"

"That bag belongs to Captain Law's daughter."

"How do you know that?"

"Look here." Leoni held a lacy handkerchief embroidered with the initials LL.

Much to Sergeant Leoni's satisfaction, Lieutenant Burney was quick to take action. He put the patrol's best rider on the least worn horse with a hastily written report and sent him off at an uncertain gallop for the fort. The report described what the patrol found at El

Muerto. The young officer had closed by writing that *". . . unless and until otherwise directed I shall attempt to track the hostiles and recover the captives. Respectfully submitted, S. J. Burney, LT."*

Maddie tried not to think about the situation she found herself in now. She had lived in the West long enough to know that fear was not an option for her. She was afraid but if she let it show it might mean the end of her and Lomida both. Most of the outlaw Indians were mean and wouldn't tolerate a whiner. At least that is what Maddie had always been told.

'Why me?' she thought to herself as she tried to think straight. *'Why is it always me?'* A single tear escaped before Maddie got control of her emotions. Anger began to take the place of fear as she realized that as always it would be up to her to get out of this mess. There was no one else. Her captors had saddled a horse for Maddie while Lomida rode behind Joseph Half Man, clinging desperately to the man's waist. They rode hard, and Maddie feared that Lomida would fall off the horse. Maddie's back hurt, her arms hurt, her whole body ached. She hated sitting astride a horse, and struggled to keep her skirts down.

Half Man guided his horse alongside Maddie's to deposit Lomida in hcr lap. Maddie quickly embraced the little girl to keep her from falling to the ground.

"Maddie, where are we and what is happening?" Lomida's small body huddled close against Maddie. A tiny quiver in her voice signaled that Lomida was on the verge of collapsing in tears from the stress of the sudden attack and an overwhelming sense of fear and despair.

"Hold on, sweetheart. Your father will come and get us as soon as he can. You know he will. I always have heard that Indians admire strength and hate weakness so try to be brave." The Indians rode hard across the plain, driving the captured horses before them. A small moan escaped Lomida's tightly pressed lips.

"Lomida, how do you feel?" Maddie tried to take the girl's mind off their predicament to think of something familiar and commonplace. "How is your leg?"

"It's okay. My back hurts more. Mr. Half Man kept pulling on my arms to make sure I wasn't going to fall and it twisted my back." She giggled in spite of herself. "Miss Maddie. Isn't that a funny name? Mr. Half Man. What do you suppose that means?"

Maddie shook her head. She had no idea of the meaning of the name, and didn't think she was too interested. She just wanted out. She wanted Fort Davis. It might have not been what she had expected but it was safe.

Chapter Five

Laughter laced the sound of women's voices as the morning sun cast patterns on the sheer organdy curtains in Captain Freeman's quarters. The small group busily worked together around a large quilting frame. If one could be a bird on high, the outline of a beautiful Star of Texas was beginning to appear on the large quilting frame that separated the chattering officers' wives. Late fall breezes stirred the curtains, offering relief to what promised to be a very warm late autumn day, what some called Indian summer. Rain would be welcome but this was the time of year when clear blue skies almost never brought rain showers. Susannah Phillips wiped her neck with a delicate cream-colored tatted handkerchief, the cloth drooping from continuous usage and more wet than dry.

"I declare. Do you think winter will ever arrive? It seems to me like this heat is going to last forever. I am ready for a little cool weather." Susannah's eyes misted over as she paused, needle suspended in air while she remembered winters spent on the pond by her home in New Hampshire. Her home, that is, until she married Surgeon Holland Phillips and became a wandering soldier's gypsy wife, following him from post to post, not caring as long as the two of them and their three rambunctious boys were together. Two now, she sighed, as she thought of their eldest, grown into a fine young man recently off to West Point to get a commission for himself. He loved the ways of the military and the excitement of the life, never knowing what was next while protecting and breaking ground for new settlers.

In the West, Susannah had found there were the settlers and the pioneers. She and her family were the pioneers. They forged ahead, cleared the ground and moved on. Then the settlers came. At times she envied the staying and settling but she also knew that she could pack in a minute if her dear husband was called to a new post.

"Pass me the thread, Sally. I swear I can't keep my needle threaded long enough to get around one side of this huge star," Nettie Wordsmith said. "Whose idea was this anyway?"

"It was yours, Nettie." Laughing, Sally Freeman handed the cream-colored thread over to her friend of several years and the last two posts. In the Army, friends you lived by fast became more your family than your real family. Army friends endured the same remote posts, and they were there beside you when your real family was hundreds of miles away and a child was ill or a husband was wounded or worse yet, didn't return from an assignment. "You are the one who thought that one giant star in the center would be easier than many small stars."

Sally calmly worked her neat small stitches in the outer framework. A delicate pattern of cream circles was forming on what looked to be a plain piece of material. When she was through, the creamy lines would turn the sides of the star into exquisite piecework. Sally was known for her even stitches—ten to an inch. All the other quilters would have been jealous if it had been anybody else, but Sally was one of the kindest women any of the other wives had ever known. She was a strong woman, filled with love for her world and a peace that showed in all that she did.

For a few moments all that could be heard was the smooth sound of thread going through cloth, freshly starched petticoats rustling as the women moved in the early afternoon trying to get to their section of the quilt better, and the sound of children's voices from somewhere outside the open window.

"Well, no one asked. But if they had . . ." Nettie Wordsmith jabbed her needle through the material. "As, I was saying, I think the captain made a big mistake sending his little one to the doctors in El Paso with that hussy of a young schoolteacher as a companion. He doesn't have a lick of sense where his daughter is concerned."

"Nettie"—Sally tried to veer the subject back to quilting—"that piece of the star you are doing is wonderful."

"Oh, come on, Sally. Pretending you aren't aware of something is not going to make it go away!" Nettie stopped her quilting as she worried the thought like a burr caught in her petticoats. "Why is she here, anyway, that young teacher? If you can even call her a teacher;

she's not even trained at a normal school. Besides, she is way too pretty for her own good."

Sally knew that until Nettie finished what she had to say, there would be no peace. Sally hated for Nettie to act this way. She often hoped to be shown how to reach this woman and help her to see that her words were like a growing cancer. They ate on her very soul and Sally noticed that one of the younger wives listened carefully but with lowered eyes, plainly uncomfortable with what Nettie was saying.

Nettie hadn't always been this sharp-tongued. Sally remembered a time before Jeff Wordsmith, the post quartermaster, started to drink so badly and was passed over for promotion to major. Nettie knew no other way to hide her hurt but to hurt someone else. It made the women cough and fidget, each trying to think of a way to change the subject.

Nettie suddenly jumped up, her spool of thread falling and rolling across the floor. "Look." She ran to the window and pulled the curtain back. "What is going on?" The women quickly got to their feet as the sound of the bugle brought them all running to the front porch.

Chapter Six

Captain John Law sat in his office enjoying the cool, early morning air, yet he knew that soon the fall heat would settle on the post like it had before the first frost came on the tobacco and cotton fields he had grown up with in his home state, North Carolina. His life had taken a direction no one could have foreseen. He remembered a time and a place and a way of life far different from the one events had thrust upon him.

When the war for southern independence broke out, John Law had rushed to join one of the first volunteer cavalry regiments formed in Salisbury, North Carolina. He'd listened to stump speakers urging boys to "jine" up for the war, for the South, and a chance at glory. "Hurry up, boys, for it'll be over in only a few weeks." He was just a country boy, looking for a little excitement. He found plenty of excitement but never saw any glory.

During a skirmish with Yankee cavalry near Port Royal, Virginia, in December of 1862 his mount was shot from under him. Taken prisoner and placed aboard a Union Navy steamer at nearby Aquia Creek, he debarked at Governors Island, New York. After a brief stay he and other Confederate prisoners were eventually transported by train to a prisoner of war camp at Elmira, New York. For sheer human cruelty, Elmira became as close to hell on Earth as any man could imagine. Located on a point bar in the bend of a small river, a board enclosure some twelve feet high entirely surrounded Elmira Camp. High on the outside of the enclosure Yankee guards patrolled a catwalk where they could see a line—"the dead line"—some fifteen or twenty feet on the inside of the enclosure. If prisoners approached the line they were shot without warning. Snow several feet deep covered the place.

Prisoners lived in slab-sided shacks some seventy or eighty feet long with light showing through gaps in the slabs. There was only one thin blanket for each man. The prisoners' quarters were searched every day, and any extra blankets were taken away. Rations were poor. In the morning each prisoner received a small piece of meat, either salt pork or pickled beef, while in the afternoon a small piece of bread usually accompanied a tin plate of so-called "soup," with sometimes a little rice or Irish potato in the water where the pork or beef had been boiled. Dysentery, pneumonia, and other illnesses were rampant. After six months of such confinement, one of every four men died. Law became desperate to escape.

During those years, in spite of the Civil War, or perhaps because of it, the numbers of Americans migrating westward increased significantly. That migration led to more contact with Indians. The large numbers of whites settling on Indian lands quickly resulted in open, bloody war on the frontier.

The Union struggled to find enough soldiers to fill its armies in the east and could spare few for frontier duty in spite of demands from settlers. To appease them President Lincoln authorized the recruitment of any Confederate prisoners who would volunteer for frontier outpost duty. After the men swore an oath of allegiance and became Union soldiers, they would be pardoned, rebels no longer. They were then shipped off to the frontier to fight Indians. Many former rebels felt that anything would be better than Elmira's certain slow death.

Because of their change of allegiance, a Yankee sergeant commented that the volunteers were like iron buckets that had an outside coating of zinc to make them rust-free, but the inside remained unchanged, a process called galvanizing. Sergeant John Law, late of the CSA, became a "Galvanized Yankee."

Duty on the frontier was difficult, but satisfying. Law worked hard over the years to earn his promotion to sergeant of U.S. Cavalry at Fort Clark, Texas. He took a patrol and trailed some Comanche raiders with two captive white children to the Mexican border near Del Rio, where he crossed the border without orders. Law and an interpreter, each armed with two massive Walker .44 caliber revolvers, met with the Indians as if they intended to buy the captives, and when Law got the children in custody the two men shot their way out of the Indian camp. Near the border Mexican cavalry intercepted Law but he bluffed his way to freedom when he told the Mexican captain that they were private citizens recently released from the Army. The

Mexican did not intend to shoot it out with crazy Texans and allowed them to pass; but his report resulted in an international incident, and the Mexican government filed a protest at the U.S. embassy.

Impressed by the boldness and courage of the former rebel, Colonel Ranald Mackenzie of the 4th U.S. Cavalry Regiment spoke on Law's behalf to General Sheridan. He argued that Law didn't deserve to be punished, but rather his kind of brassy initiative, lacking in many frontier Army officers at the time, deserved to be rewarded. "General," Mackenzie roared, "you know I've taken my men across that border myself, and I'll do it again if need be!" His argument prevailed, and Sheridan called in a few political debts and arranged for Law to quietly receive a commission as a second lieutenant. While it was illegal for a Galvanized Yankee ex-Confederate to become a commissioned officer in the Yankee Army, Sheridan got his way. So much had happened since then.

His pipe rested on the top of a stack of papers that seemed to never end. John loved the Army and his duty, but at what expense did he serve? He looked at one of the two pictures he kept on his desk. Vivian, her lovely face forever frozen in solemn repose, sat for the Daguerre process likeness. The eyes seemed to look right at him and he gently used his kerchief to wipe the ever-present West Texas dust from the frame. He remembered Vivian, so young, so happy, and so full of life. So in love with him once that she never questioned leaving all that she knew and was comfortable with; for years Vivian was eager to go with him whenever John received orders to a new post. She gladly followed him from post to post. However, his last posting to Fort Davis had been far away from Vivian's idea of civilization. She was not interested in the clear skies, the cool, dry mornings, and the vivid sunrises that made the post so attractive; she wanted more.

Vivian began to be restless for shops, for dances, for the theatre, for the things that big cities had to offer. Restlessness had come over her and while John knew she loved him, he also realized that she was developing a rebellious streak that threatened to overwhelm her. He had seen it coming and been helpless to do anything about it. Vivian wanted to stay later at the parties, wanted to be transferred to one of the large Army posts near a city.

John had warned her about Thunder. Thunder was a horse that had been ridden by a government contract horse wrangler, who believed the first step in training a horse was to break his spirit. John bought the horse at an Army auction when he was declared an outlaw after he nearly killed a cavalryman. Thunder stood seventeen hands high and was black with a long scar across his flank.

At Fort Clark, John met a man called Jim Sam Webster, an Uvalde wrangler who knew his horses. Jim Sam told John to try "side-lining" that horse, tie him to a tame horse that wouldn't wander out of camp and run off. Jim Sam believed in side-lining, and said he'd have side-lined his wild youngest daughter if he could have found a tame girl to tie her to. John knew he should listen to the man, meant to take the time to work with the horse, and had the time to do it right. However, before John could finish working with the animal, Vivian had decided to ride him. She had taken Lomida and gone riding when

John was out on a routine patrol. She had known not to go, but thought she could handle the animal.

A search party found Vivian dead, her neck broken, with Lomida pinned underneath her, alive but her right leg was broken and twisted. Everyone assumed the horse had shied; perhaps he had seen a snake, but in truth no one would ever know. Lomida didn't remember. All anyone knew was that the horse had returned to the post limping and had to be destroyed.

John had been the one exposed to all the danger and risk. Not Vivian. He mourned the younger Vivian he had lost to the prairies and the vastness of the open spaces and whatever sickness it was that took such a toll on her mind. People thought he looked at Lomida and mourned Vivian, but John knew that when he looked at Lomida he was filled with anger for the Vivian who had allowed his only child to be injured in such a manner. That much anger is a hard thing to reconcile to but John was working on it.

Carefully, he replaced Vivian's picture and rejoiced as he picked up Lomida's picture. When it was taken he stood behind the photographer while his little girl, chafing at the enforced rigidity of the pose, smiled at him. The sepia photograph couldn't show her blue eyes and dark red hair. She was constantly losing her hat and so freckles dotted her nose and cheeks. She definitely looked more like her mother than him. Vivian's family came from Ireland and she and Lomida had inherited the fair, sensitive skin associated with many Irish. John's complexion was dark with brown hair and hazel eyes. Tall and lean, he came from a family where height was the norm. Except for his friend Tilman, he had always been the tallest boy in school.

Thoughts of Vivian's death usually brought his old friend Tilman to mind. Law remembered years before when he and Tilman grew up together in the same community, both reared on family farms located across Lyle's Creek from each other. When John was twelve years old he pulled Tilman out of the rain-swollen creek where they trapped muskrats and otters. Tilman had been a couple of years older and very embarrassed. The two had sworn a childish oath to always help each other in danger or trouble. John had been so excited that he had done the saving that he still chuckled when he thought about the escapade. Tilman had always bragged he was the better swimmer, but not after that.

Tilman married Sarah, his childhood sweetheart, while John married Vivian, the only girl he had ever loved. Now, only he and Tilman remained.

After the Civil War, Tilman moved to Texas and settled near Packsaddle Mountain, west of Austin. He was trying to make a go of it running a few cattle. But then Tilman's wife was killed by Indians and he became a hard, unforgiving man. John took leave to go to help Tilman, to offer whatever comfort he could. Tilman had been glad to see him but was so immersed in his misery and loss that he had not been able to receive help. John said nothing when he learned that Tilman sent his only son Dan to work for his keep in Fredericksburg and Tilman, seething with anger, rode to avenge Sarah.

When Vivian died, Tilman stood by John, although he was a much different man. Cold and afraid to let go, his hatred had made him feared in parts of Texas. Even though his manner was brusque and distant, just his being there helped hold John together as they buried

Vivian. John and Lomida were left to be on their own, as Tilman was left with his son Dan. John needed the strength Tilman offered.

A few months back, Dan, working for a stage line, was bushwhacked and shot dead. A short letter came from Tilman stating he was in Colorado looking for the man who murdered Dan. A sigh escaped John's lips. Life turned out much differently than either planned.

John prepared to deal with the paper work that was a post adjutant's lot—unit returns, supply vouchers, pay vouchers for civilian contract workers, and the countless other forms an Army generates—when he heard a disturbance outside his door. The sound of a galloping horse being pulled to a quick stop brought John back to the present. His first thought was, why didn't that rider stop at the dismount point? Voices rose in an excited exchange followed by the sound of hurried footsteps.

Sharp knocks sounded at his door. "Come!"

First Sergeant Eamon Duncannon, pushed into John's office, his weathered face plainly distressed, and began to speak. "Cap'n, one of Mr. Burney's lads has something to report." He stepped aside as the trooper approached the captain's desk, clutching the two objects retrieved from the stagecoach in his dusty hands, halted, and saluted.

Law returned the salute. "Report, Trooper." Dread paralyzed John. Lomida. He knew.

The trooper handed John the hastily written note from Lieutenant Burney along with two items John immediately recognized—Maddie Brown's hat, a prized favorite she always wore to the promenades at the fort, the once bright red ribbons that went around the brim now dirty and tattered, and a small crocheted burgundy purse. Law opened the purse knowing that he would find a faded picture of his wife. Lomida never had one without the other. "Where . . ."

Law read the note, looked up at the trooper standing at attention before his desk, and the man began his story . . .

Chapter Seven

By the time the trooper finished his tale, John's mind raced with questions—what could he do? How, and with what? Almost all of the fort's able-bodied men were with Colonel Grierson, who had taken both the cavalry and the infantry regiments on patrol, mapping and guarding water holes while looking for Apaches away up in southern New Mexico. The few men left at the post, aside from the casuals—the sick and the shirkers—would be little help. He couldn't order them into Mexico, and the Indians almost always took their white captives across the border to sell. Everyone on the frontier was aware that most captives were never returned and those who showed up years later, especially women, were shunned by all and usually had trouble readjusting to life as they had known it before. In fact, the Indians may have killed Lomida and Miss Maddie already.

Law, as senior officer of the line present on the post, was acting post commander. He was bound by his oath as an officer to carry out his duties first and foremost. Even before family. He spat a curse, frustrated that the only possibility of quick rescue depended on an untested officer only recently arrived from the East.

"Leoni's with him, sir," Duncannon reminded Law. "He's one of the best soldiers in the regiment. If anybody can help right now, he's the one."

Law suppressed his anger and, outwardly at least, regained the calm manner that made him respected in the rough and ready frontier cavalry; until Burney's men returned to report, he had to do something. He decided on his first action. Send for Tilman Wagner. He would come. John pulled a sheet of paper from a desk drawer, reached for a pen, dipped it in ink, and began writing. The only sound in the room was the scratching of his pen on paper.

Tilman Wagner
Stone's Boarding House
Mahonville, Colorado

Lomida and schoolteacher captured by Indians.
Need help now. Come quick.

John Law
Fort Davis, Texas

He folded the paper and handed it to Duncannon. "First Sar'nt, get this over to the telegraph office, and then get this trooper a hot meal and some rest." He looked at the young soldier. "Good report. Dismissed."

Chapter Eight

They had ridden hard for hours into the twilight at the tail end of the day. They stopped at a small water hole hidden among large boulders at the foot of a steep hill, and the small horse herd was bunched in a dry wash. One of the raiders killed a mule and now squatted by a fire to roast some of the meat.

"Oh, Miss Maddie, my leg feels like it's on fire." Lomida rubbed her injured leg. It was smaller than the other one and very thin. An ugly red welt showed where her leg had beat helplessly on the saddle as she and Maddie had ridden at the breakneck speed of the raiders. Lomida had a great deal of trouble trying to control the weakened muscles in the injured leg. That was the reason she and Maddie had been going to El Paso. A doctor there was reputed to be almost miraculous with withered limbs.

Maddie and Lomida rested on the ground by a saddle in the shadows some yards away from the fire. Maddie had no idea where they were, and even if they had been free to roam they could go nowhere. Lomida had little strength left after the day's ride and besides, Maddie couldn't leave her even if she knew where to go.

The sky was still light blue in the west, but faded quickly as darkness grew and stars began to fill the sky. Maddie saw that soon it would be fully dark, and she feared the night. Who knew what they would be up against?

Fear took her back to the early years after her parents were killed on the way to Kansas. Independence, Missouri, had many wonderful things for people to see and do, but Maddie knew Independence only from the inside of the orphanage in which she had been placed. For four years that was her life. She was a young girl, alone and far too pretty for her own good.

Many a night she had catnapped in the darkness, clutching a fork stolen from the dining hall in her hand, while listening for the approach of one of the older boys. There were a bold few who wanted to get too friendly. The memory brought a grim smile briefly to her lips. Several of them were marked for life by long scars on their arms and hands, but none had said anything because they would have been in trouble with the old man who ran the orphanage. In fact, Maddie thought, the old man himself had a scar on his leg to remember her by. She was under no misapprehension that the savages who had taken her captive would be so easily discouraged by any resistance she could offer.

The leader of the Indians came near Maddie and spoke harshly. He gestured for Joseph Half Man to come. He spoke again, and this time Joseph translated.

"Whips His Horse say why girl's leg not right?"

Before Maddie could answer Whips His Horse

touched her hair, pulled a long pale braid, and tugged harder.

Maddie bit her lip hard to hold back the cry of pain.

"Whips His Horse say hair like waterfall, worth much whiskey, many horses."

Whips His Horse smiled wickedly, turned, and yelled at the small group of raiders who sat a few yards away from the girls. They listened, nodded, and turned to face the fire.

"He say no man touch woman or girl."

Maddie was certain that Whips His Horse was a cold-blooded man. What reason would he have for leaving her alone?

"Now, lady. What happen to this leg?" Joseph sat down by Maddie, curiously examining Lomida's twisted limb. "Bad leg no good. Leave girl for wolves and coyotes." He laughed cruelly as he watched Lomida try to draw her leg under her dirty gown. The red plaid taffeta had been her pride and joy but now the skirt was caked with dirt and spots of blood. Lomida tried to move closer to Maddie, keeping her head down, unconsciously twisting her hands together as she held her breath. Joseph leaned nearer to Lomida, plainly enjoying her discomfort. Lomida flinched. The man smelled of unwashed clothing and stank of stale sweat.

Once again Joseph poked Lomida on the leg, hard enough to hurt, and smiled when she made a sound of protest. "Leg not good, little one, but hair like dark fire in winter." Pulling a strand of hair around to Lomida's anxious face, he smiled. "Old men see red hair and youth, not care that part of you no good." His laugh seemed both vicious and evil at the same time. "Pay much."

"We need water," Maddie demanded with a boldness

which came from Whips His Horse's edict that they be
left untouched. "We want to wash, and we want to
drink."

"You come drink mescal. You sleep my blanket,"
Joseph leered.

Maddie had heard that mescal was a potent drink,
fermented cactus juice, and she wanted none of it.
Thirst was nothing compared to what happened when
the mescal took over. "No. I am not that thirsty." It took
everything she had to say that and turn away from the
man as she had not had a drink all day except for early
in the morning when they had first begun to ride.

Lomida needed water; the girl continually attempted
to wet her already chapped lips. Maddie turned back to
Joseph. She wouldn't beg but for Lomida she would
humble herself a little bit. "The little one isn't used to
going without water."

"Water for girl." Joseph pointed to a place in the
rocks where Maddie could find water.

He left her and went to the fire, squatted, produced a
large knife and sliced off a strip of mule meat and
began to eat with obvious relish.

Maddie took a canteen from the saddle, filled it, and
let Lomida sip the cool water. The evening breeze
brought a chill, and before the night was over Maddie
and Lomida would be cold. Lomida quickly fell asleep
curled next to Maddie, softly sighing in her sleep.
Lomida had been overprotected all her life, but she had
not complained the whole day and that said a lot for her
character and upbringing. It had been a frightening day
and who knew what would become of them. Maddie
tried to stretch out the best she could knowing she also

needed rest. Unfortunately, sleep evaded her as her mind wouldn't settle down.

Stars flamed blue-white, some were yellow, another blood red. They seemed almost close enough to touch in the dark sky above. The last light of the day showed that her new hunter's green dress had become a dusty gray color. Maddie had saved up to buy the material at the Fort Davis Mercantile and she had spent many evenings patiently stitching and re-stitching the material. The officers' wives had a sewing group but she knew that she was not welcome. In fact, she was considered to be trouble by many of the ladies. A young attractive woman with no family or husband was whispered about on a military post, especially by the other women. Sally Freeman always spoke politely to Maddie but she had never been invited to her home.

When she sewed she was very thankful for the time she had spent in Dodge City, Kansas, with the Johnsons when she had worked in their dry goods store. A kindly old lady, Mrs. Johnson had been scandalized to learn that the orphanage had taught Maddie few skills, so she had taken it upon herself to teach the young woman basic sewing; how to cut a pattern from newspaper and how to pin and sew and measure. Very proud of her new green dress, Maddie once hoped it would help her to find a new position in El Paso.

While Lomida was under the doctor's care, Maddie intended to see if she could find a place of good repute to hire her. A saloon was out of the question—El Paso was rumored to have more than fifty of them—but she could work in a dry goods store if needed. She liked working with numbers and had enjoyed studying mathematics books left at the school by the previous teacher.

Lomida stirred. Maddie tried to cover her as best she could. Whips had given them nothing to use for cover or to sleep on so Maddie tried to use the long full skirt on her dress to cover Lomida's legs as well as her own. Lomida was fragile in many ways and she didn't need the illness that could come from their harsh situation. Lomida had a lot of spunk for a little girl. Sometimes Maddie thought that they got along well since they had both lost their mothers at a young age. If wishes were free Maddie would not wish to leave Lomida. It would be cruel of her to escape alone and let Lomida's father down, for he trusted her with Lomida's safety.

Captain Law was still involved with his dead wife as far as Maddie could tell. He had escorted Maddie to a promenade several times around the post but she knew he was only being polite. When Maddie thought about John Law, she wondered whether she would like to get to know him better. He seemed a good and temperate man; certainly he was pleasant to look at. His hair was light brown and he had hazel eyes that rarely smiled but studied the world around him. Lomida's red hair must have come from her mother. John Law was what she imagined the prince would look like in the fairy tales she read to her students. She laughed quietly; it must be the night air, giving her such foolish thoughts. Maddie Brown and the captain of Fort Davis. Not likely! A first quarter moon was rising in the east. It was time to be realistic and to go to sleep; in truth, neither she nor Lomida would probably ever see him again. The morning would bring a new set of troubles and she needed to be prepared.

Chapter Nine

The Atchison, Topeka and Santa Fe Railroad passenger coach had seen much hard use. The once-plush red velvet upholstered seats, stained and worn, were small and too close together, and at six foot three inches tall Tilman Wagner found small comfort only by leaning back against the window and stretching his legs toward the aisle. The window acted as a mirror; beneath the familiar big hat the face that stared back at Tilman seemed to have more lines than he remembered. There was even more gray in the beard stubble where there had been little, or so it seemed to him.

South of Trinidad the train made a slow and laborious climb up snow-blanketed Raton Pass, for the snows had started early. After passing the crest the train then crept slowly down to the town of Raton in New Mexico Territory. Picking up speed the train easily made its way south across an open, grassy prairie south toward Santa Fe. To the west the snow-capped rampart of the Rocky Mountains thrust high into the clear blue skies.

The moaning of strong cold wind gusts from the mountains buffeted the coach and could be heard above the clatter of the rails. Tilman felt an involuntary shiver, for he'd experienced the bone-aching cold of those mountains when the wind drove heavy snow before it.

The trip had been unexpected and Tilman felt pushed into it. Several months back Tilman had arrived in Mahonville, Colorado, searching for his only son's killer. While there he found the killer, got slightly wounded in a shootout, and found Catherine Stone. Tilman had hoped for more time to sort out some things. Most important, what were his intentions towards Catherine? That was not to be, at least not yet. An urgent telegram arrived from his old friend John Law asking for help. The man had once saved Tilman's life, and he could not refuse; he packed hastily and set out alone the very next day.

He hoped the trouble would be over by the time he got to Texas, but he knew a little about West Texas, with its miles and miles of unsettled land in which renegades, border jumpers and Apaches could hide. From the time white men moved into central Texas and came into contact with Comanche Indians there had been kidnappings of young women and children. Sometimes the captives were dragged down the Comanche War Trail to Mexico and sold. There they became old men's playthings or worse. Tilman knew little about Apaches, only that they were fierce warriors who preferred to fight afoot in their rugged mountain and canyon homelands.

The caboose on the South Arkansas to Pueblo work train on which he started his trip had had a wood-burning stove and hot coffee, but hard bench seats. There simply was no easy way to travel, and since leaving San Antonio for Colorado—what was it, four months back?—Tilman had done a sight of it. He reached for the telegram in his pocket and winced. The place where a bullet hit him was still tender.

"Still a-hurtin', ol' hoss?"

Tilman's mouth dropped open as Butter Pegram tossed saddlebags into the overhead luggage rack and sat down across from him, tilting his hat back with a big grin.

"Butter!"

"I thought you could use a friend. Kinda got used to you an' your shenanigans an' I figured you was a lot more interestin' than most of the people in Mahonville. Besides, I wanted to make sure that you didn't get in no trouble. Miss Catherine wouldn't like that none a-tall."

Tilman snorted, asking before he could stop himself, "Did you see Catherine before you left? How is James doing? How . . ."

"Hold on, there, pard. You ain't been gone from there but a day!" Butter laughed. "Catherine sent you this note and James added a line or two as well." Butter handed over a small note that smelled of lavender, like Catherine. "I'm hungry. Think I'll go get shed of this chawin' tobaccy." Butter rolled a dark brown lump from one cheek to the other. "I brought along some chuck Catherine packed. Be right back."

Tilman smiled as Butter lumbered unsteadily down the aisle, trying to find the rhythm of the coach. A real friend, Butter knew that Tilman wanted privacy to read his letter.

Dear Tilman,
    Hope the trip is going well and by the time you get to Texas your friend has his daughter safely

home. Butter is determined that you need his help and I think that is just fine. We already miss you here in Mahonville. I learned today that there will be a real election for mayor next month.

You left some things and I have put them away until you return to get them. Please hurry back. You are missed very much.
Take care, Catherine

A small note was enclosed from James as well.

Mister Tilman, we mis you. I cott a big fish. Be careful. James

Tilman folded the note and put it in his pocket. He'd read it again later. He had left in such a hurry he really didn't know how he felt about Catherine. She was a fine woman and had been helpful when he needed a friend. But facts being what they were, she was settled in Colorado while he was off to Texas with no idea what might happen to him there. *Please hurry back. You are missed very much*, she had written. How would he answer that and be fair to her? Was it right for either of them to build hopes at a time like this? What kind of future could he offer her?

"You daydreamin'? You ain't sick, are you?" Butter reclaimed his seat across from Tilman. "Hey, what's goin' on with the two of you if you don't mind me a-stickin' my big nose in? Pastor Fry said you all looked 'mighty friendly' the day you left. What'd he mean?" Butter grumbled, cautiously watching Tilman.

Yesterday's parting came back to him as if it was happening all over again.

"Tilman, wait." Catherine hurried over to Tilman as he started out the door, his saddlebags and bedroll in hand. "Do you have any idea when you'll return?" She paused, placed a hand on his arm. "You will be returning won't you?"

Tilman studied her face, aware of the warmth of her touch. It felt so right to him. "I'll be back as soon as I help John find Lomida." He shifted his weight, suddenly hesitant. "Maybe she will be home already and this trip will be for nothing. But, I have to go."

"I never thought otherwise, Tilman Wagner. Just don't forget me or James, please."

Tilman dropped his gear and pulled Catherine to him, something he had wanted to do for weeks, and kissed her soundly on the lips.

Words seemed to fail Catherine as she looked helplessly into Tilman's eyes, her expression speaking volumes. "Tilman."

"Hummm. Excuse me, folks." Pastor Fry stood at the end of the hallway with Catherine's son James, both of them wearing delighted expressions.

Tilman released Catherine, and nodded. Truth be told, he didn't trust his own voice, for he didn't want to squeak like a boy who'd just stolen his first schoolyard kiss.

Composed, he managed to say, "Howdy, Pastor."

Catherine looked elated as Tilman picked up his bags and walked to his horse, tied his gear on the saddle and climbed aboard.

"James, pick up my horse at the station, remember?"

With that, Tilman turned and rode off down the road towards the town.

He cleared his throat. "Catherine is a fine woman, Butter." Tilman paused as he searched for the right words. "A mighty fine woman. But I've got to help John." Tilman changed the subject. "Did I hear you say you brought food?"

Butter untied a cloth bundle he'd placed on the seat to reveal two dozen of Catherine's yeast rolls stuffed with thick slices of beef, and what seemed to be fudge wrapped in waxed paper. "Boy, this sure beats freezing atop a stagecoach, don't it?"

Suddenly hungry, Tilman quickly agreed and reached for the bundle.

"Butter, thanks for siding me in this."

"Tell me about this man, Tilman. I need a idee of what to expect." The train's wheels clicked across rail joints in endless monotony. Tilman stretched his long legs out in the side aisle as he considered how to answer Butter.

"John Law and I grew up together in North Carolina. Our families had the two largest farms in the county until the war. We were the youngest boys in our families, and he was younger than me by a couple of years. Came the war, and when we went off to fight we were still not full grown. You know what the war was like."

Butter nodded.

"Anyway, after I got paroled I walked home. Between Yankee occupation and reconstruction the place was ruined, our farms burned, family living like dogs. We had no money, no chance of making any, for the carpetbaggers taxed us all to death to steal the land."

Butter fished around in his pocket, produced a pocketknife and his plug of tobacco, cut off a chaw, popped it in his mouth, and settled to hear more.

"John was already in Texas. He was captured in '62, near died in Elmira prison camp way up north, so he got 'galvanized.'" Some held that against him, but I never did. A man's got to live, and doing nothing he'd have gone under for sure. Well sir, like so many of the boys, that old restless spirit come over me." Tilman paused to watch the prairie slip past the window.

Butter nodded. He knew what Tilman was talking about.

"So I decided to go to Texas. John and I were both married by then to our childhood sweethearts and so it became a grand adventure." Tilman paused at the recollection. "Growing up, it was always John and Vivian and me and Sarah. I took land out west of Austin; Dan came along, and we saw it as a challenge. John and Vivian stayed in the Army and they had a little girl. Lomida is named after my dead wife, Sarah Lomida Wagner. Anyway, things were fine for a while. Vivian always loved horses and was a good rider.

"John went to Fort Davis in '70, barely three years after Indian attacks on the mail road caused the reopening of the fort. Two years later Vivian was out riding with Lomida. The horse shied or something and threw the two of them. Vivian must have tried to protect the girl and got trampled. Lomida has one leg off-kilter as a result of the accident and John has never been the same."

Tilman hesitated, lost in thought, and then continued. "You know, Butter, it was odd. When I went to Fort Davis for the funeral John told me that right before Vivian died she got real homesick for society and life someplace other than on a small Army post in the middle of nowhere. He said he had asked her not to ride the horse she was on since it was known to be hard-headed."

"You and John had the dangerous jobs and you're both still here but your wives are gone. Many a feller loses a wife in childbirth, but it's uncommon what happened to y'all."

The west winds quieted, and in the almost empty car the constant clicking sounds of the tracks became part of the silence, and lulled them near sleep as each thought about Tilman's story. And now, where was Lomida?

Chapter Ten

"Santa Fe, folks, Santa Fe." The conductor made his way through the cars. "Last stop."

"You awake, Butter?" Tilman coughed, cleared his throat. "We're here."

The train crept into a newly constructed station built after the Spanish style of mud-coated adobe bricks. Tilman and Butter stepped from the car and stretched, stiff from hours of inactivity. Several groups of children watched from the streets out front of the station, as close as their courage would take them, full of wide-eyed wonder at the noisy, smoking locomotive. The whistle shrieked once and the kids covered their ears, retreated a few steps, and then laughed as their courage returned.

Tilman picked up his saddlebags and bedroll while Butter gathered his gear and lifted Catherine's small picnic bundle. "Lighter than it was." Butter chuckled. "I'm right hungry again."

"Already?"

"I learned the hard way a man should eat when he can get it. Never know when you might have nothing."

After a short walk to the stage station, they learned that luck was with them. A talkative agent wearing sleeve garters and a green eyeshade told them that the weekly stage going south was scheduled to leave around midnight. After they bought their tickets to Mesilla, down by the Mexican border, the agent recommended a nearby saloon that laid out a fair bait of grub.

Tilman and Butter walked along San Francisco Street, pausing to gawk in the windows of Spiegellberg Brothers store before continuing around the main plaza to stretch their legs. Near the old Spanish governor's palace Indians from some of the pueblos around Santa Fe sat on colorful blankets and displayed fine silver rings and jewelry for sale. Tilman enjoyed the feel of the crisp fall air as he and Butter stopped to look at some of the wares. A small but exquisitely crafted cross inlaid with vibrant turquoise caught Tilman's eye. It would please Catherine, he thought, so after a bit of haggling, he bought it. The vendor placed it in a small, beaded buckskin bag with a drawstring.

"Who's that for? Ain't Pastor Fry got enough crosses?" Butter chided.

"Let's go eat." Tilman hastily pocketed his prize. "I'm hungry and you need something to put in your mouth. That's obvious!"

Spanish Santa Fe reminded Tilman in many ways of San Antonio. "Maybe it's the food," Tilman thought out loud.

"What say? You started talking to yourself again?"

"You got me." Tilman laughed. "Thinking about

food. I'm hungry enough to eat a steer by myself, hoof, horn, and hide!"

They stood in front of an adobe hotel called La Fonda. The streets teemed with a noisy crowd of Mexicans, Americans, and several buckskin-clad men weaving among burros and two-wheeled ox carts loaded with all manner of goods. Well-dressed gents with their ladies passed them at the entrance, as did several blue-uniformed officers.

"Yankee soldiers must belong to the territorial governor's staff," Tilman commented to Butter. Tilman read a sign out front that said the hotel had been there over two hundred years, since the early days of the Spanish settlement in America. He could also see that the hotel had its own restaurant. The smell of roasting green chiles wafted on the breeze. The door to the restaurant stood open and Tilman heard the sounds of plates clinking, people talking, and decided to go inside.

"No telling what kind of grub we'll find on the road, so let's grab a good bite while we can."

The two men passed through the tall iron-bound wooden doors into the cool and dark interior. In the restaurant, they were seated at a small round table, the top covered in tanned cowhide. The chairs had cowhide on the seats and were wicker. After he ordered Tilman looked around at the adobe walls. Butter pointed out a colorfully painted mural of fandango dancers on one long wall; the surroundings combined with the high-altitude breezes to make it a pleasant place.

Their meal arrived and the hungry men waded into bowls of spicy green chili and venison stew. "Tilman," Butter said as he dabbed beads of sweat off his upper lip, "what do you make of this stew?" Butter motioned for the waiter to bring more water. "What's in this?" He emptied his glass in one long gulp.

"Eat a tortilla and quit bellyaching, Butter." Tilman laughed. The stew was the *picante* version, with plenty of green chiles and small pieces of meat. "It bites back, but sure tastes good." He downed a glass of water as well. "I could eat it every day, I think."

"If you did, you wouldn't have a tongue left in a year." Butter drank another glass of water and hiccupped. "Aw, dang!" He hiccupped again.

At midnight the southbound stage pulled out and the two men were once again on the road that would take them to Fort Davis. From Santa Fe they traveled rough and dusty roads across broken country unseen in the darkness. After a meal stop in Albuquerque two drummers boarded the stage and carried on a lively conversation about the Lincoln County Wars. One of the men speculated that Territory Governor Axtell was involved with some outfit called The Ring in Santa Fe. They alluded to shadowy, unnamed men in the territorial capital who were somehow connected to the war and schemed to keep the fighting going because there was money to be made. They were glad to show off their knowledge, and self-importantly talked endlessly about odd goings-on in Mesilla. Tilman had heard of the Lincoln Wars but knew little about Mesilla, and the conversations during the next two days at least helped to pass some of the time.

From the talk Tilman learned that Mesilla was a thriving adobe community of about two thousand souls, mostly Mexicans. The village rested in a desert valley southwest of the bleak and rugged peaks of the Organ Mountains. The name came from the way near-vertical, jagged granite peaks appeared to resemble the pipes of a great cathedral organ. The men said that the Anglos and Mexicans and Indians of the town got along well enough.

But, they went on to say, hard feelings still simmered among differing Anglo factions in Mesilla. Back in 1861, according to one of the drummers, boisterous political rallies, featuring bands and speakers for the Unionists and for the Secessionists, marched around the town square at the start of the Civil War and the demonstration turned ugly. In what was called "The Battle of the Bands," a shootout in the town square between the rival Republican and Democrat political factions, resulted in ten deaths and more than forty men wounded.

At one time Mesilla served as the capital of the Confederate state of Arizona. Because the people refused to forget the shooting incident and the town's role in the confederacy, a rift between residents from the northern states and those hailing from Dixie still festered, and fistfights still erupted when people talked about it. The Mexicans of Mesilla would never understand the why of it; the Indians understood it as tribal warfare, no different than the generations-old war between Navajos and Utes.

Tilman and Butter learned that they would have to wait until the following evening for the eastbound stage. Across the dusty street from the Mesilla stage station a brightly painted sign announced a large adobe building as the Corn Exchange Hotel. Upon the recommendation of one of the drummers they decided to take rooms at the Corn Exchange, so they collected their belongings and made the short walk to the hotel. Shifting his saddlebags to his left hand, Tilman reached to open the hotel door, but stepped back when the door was flung open in his face.

Chapter Eleven

"**Y**ou old bat! You can't put me out of my room and expect me to pay too!" A man, pistol in hand, was backing out of the hotel's doorway, and over the man's shoulder Tilman caught a glimpse of a frightened woman standing in front of the hotel desk with her hands in the air. *What kind of western man is this who'd throw down on a woman?* Tilman quickly drew his Colt .45 and placed the muzzle against the man's head, cocking the hammer back. At the sudden cold hardness behind his ear and the ominous click, cli-click sounds of a hammer thumbed back and a trigger setting, the man froze.

"Drop it," Tilman said in a low voice.

A gun clattered to the floor. "Don't shoot; you got the bulge on me."

"Back on out, slowly. If I stumble you'll be shaking hands with the Devil."

"I'm coming."

"Butter, see if you can find the city marshal," Tilman

said, taking a good look at the man before him. He held his gun on a youngish fellow, probably no more than sixteen or seventeen years old, stinking of whiskey. That explained why he'd draw on a woman.

"No need, I'm right here," a voice came from behind Tilman. "You boys just hold it right there."

The woman from the hotel stepped out the door just then, somewhat calmer than when Tilman had last seen her. "Chet," she spoke to the marshal, "that cowboy came in drunk and busted up his room, and you know Mr. Davis would never allow that in our hotel when he was alive. Then he went and disturbed my other customers, threatened one of them for complaining. I tried to make him leave, but he wouldn't, and when I insisted, why, he had the gall to pull a gun on me! I'm a poor widow just trying to get by." All at once she was near tears.

"Now, Missus Davis," the marshal said, "it's all right. He's headed for the lockup. The judge'll see to it he pays for damages and he won't bother you again." Chet shoved the now remorseful young cowboy down the street.

Turning to Tilman and Butter, the lady smiled wanly. "Thank you both for helping me. Come inside, please." She stepped back into the lobby of the hotel where several guests were drifting back to their rooms now that the excitement was over. "I'm Augustina Davis. John, my husband, died recently and now I'm running our hotel by myself. Thank you for helping me out."

"Glad to oblige," Tilman said, taking off his hat. "We'd like rooms for the night if you have any."

"I'll tell you what, you boys can stay here anytime you want, no charge."

"Ma'am, we'll pay. We don't want to take advantage," Butter said.

"I insist. It's little enough I can do to thank you."

Tilman and Butter later discovered that Augustina Davis was a stern and capable worker, for she not only ran the hotel, but a restaurant in the same adobe, as well as several other businesses she and her late husband had started or purchased. They were delighted to learn that in Augustina's restaurant they dined free. They managed to eat their fill of green chile stew—the locally grown chiles seemed especially tasty—and Butter satisfied his sweet tooth with several bags of sugared, roasted pecans.

After supper they strolled around the square enjoying the evening, admired the San Albino Catholic Church that fronted on the square, and stopped in a saloon for a drink to get caught up on the local doings. The bar talk was all about the trial of one of the participants in the Lincoln County War, and Tilman listened carefully. A chatty barkeep, eager to show off his take on the recent legal wrangling at the county seat, took it upon himself to enlighten the two strangers. It seems that Susan McSween, wife of Alex McSween, a man who was killed in the Five-Days Battle during the Lincoln County War up to the north and east of Mesilla, hired a lawyer named Chapman and charged one Nathan A. M. Dudley with the arson of her home. However, Lawyer Chapman turned up murdered before the trial and everybody was saying that it was Dudley who hired the killing. Susan McSween had come to Mesilla the previous week for the trial, but after three days Dudley was acquitted and released, so she left town. Tongues still wagged. A Texas cowboy at the bar listened, and when the barkeep finished his story, offered his own opinion of what happened.

"I'd say that McSween died on account of he had defective vision."

"How's that?"

"Well, somebody with a gun saw McSween before McSween saw him! His eyes was defective, don't you know?"

After a good knee-slapping laugh up and down the bar, talk went on to other men, other places. The Texan went into a long-winded story about a man he knew who had nothing but bad luck, however Tilman and Butter were no longer listening.

"Well," an uncharacteristically somber Butter said to Tilman after hearing as much war talk as he could stand, "I read some about that war, an' you and me have been in one; I reckon war's good business for gravediggers, an' good for making many a widow an' a orphan." He refilled his glass. "I'm sorry for that widow McSween, but if that feller Dudley's acquitted it sounds to me like she was left with nothing but a whole lot of 'she-said' and 'he-said,'" Butter observed, staring into his drink. "I've said m' piece." He tossed off his whiskey.

From others in the saloon Tilman heard stories of Apache troubles along the stage route they would be taking, so after finishing his drink he visited a gunsmith.

"I've heard of this gun," he said to Butter as he admired a Winchester Model 1876 rifle, "I figure a good long arm might come in handy out in the desert." The rifle had a long range flip-up peep sight mounted on the stock behind the receiver and was chambered for a .45–75 cartridge, a .45 slug pushed along by seventy-five grains of black powder. The soft lead slug weighed 350 grains and packed considerable stopping power well out beyond five hundred yards. Tilman bought the rifle, and five twenty-round boxes of cartridges. The gunsmith threw in an extra box for free.

After watching Tilman, Butter decided on a Model 73 carbine in .44-40 caliber.

"A wise choice, my friend," the gunsmith said, "as I see your belt gun is also a .44."

"If I can see a man I can hit him. An' if I hit that feller this'll stop him, just like my handgun, an' this 'un won't bust my shoulder a-doin' it."

The next morning they walked outside of town a ways where they tested the rifles and adjusted the sights. At dinner a more composed and relaxed Augustina joined them for coffee, and said that Chet had come by with the money for the room damages, and told her that the cowboy would be a guest of the county for the next ninety days. Looking at Butter, she asked, "You boys be passing through here again?"

"Hard to say, but I reckon we will sometimes," Tilman answered.

"You're welcome here, don't forget." She smiled demurely while Butter squirmed, suddenly uncomfortable in his chair.

"We'd best get our stuff together," Butter suggested to Tilman. "We don't want to miss that stage this evening."

Their journey continued on to El Paso, Texas, Butter being unusually introspective.

"You know," Tilman said, "I'm kind of partial to widows myself."

Silence.

"Missus Davis was a handsome woman, well fixed so a man would never have to work."

Silence. Then, "That ain't funny. Let it be, Tilman."

Tilman was wise enough to let it be.

Later, Butter offered, "Don't know what it is about widow women an' me. Seems like one's always wanting to take me to a preaching or some such. I ain't a-going to marry no widow woman, and that's just all there is to it."

They traveled on to Fort Quitman, Van Horn's Wells and finally into the way station at Dead Man's Hole where the stage stopped to change the teams.

"I'm new around here boys. Coffee's on the stove, so help yourselves while we unhitch. They was some trouble here a week or so back and I ain't got no help yet."

Tilman realized the trouble being discussed concerned Lomida.

"Apaches raided the place, kilt the station manager and taken two girls from over to Fort Davis captive. It was a awful mess I reckon." He nervously wiped his hands on his britches. "I'd figgered to bring my wife and young'uns with me but I left them in El Paso 'til things settle down and the Army rounds up them Injuns."

The stage pulled out of Dead Man's Hole, and the new teams—rough broke mules with minds of their own—swung wide of the road causing a front wheel to hit a rock and slew into a dry wash which snapped the wheel off the axle.

"What the . . . ?" Butter jumped out and examined the wheel, his years of working the coaches in Colorado coming quickly into play as he went to help.

"Looks like this will take the rest of the day boys," the stagecoach driver muttered to his express guard as they also checked the break. "This is broke clean through. I'll have to fix up a replacement."

"We need to get on over to Fort Davis today," Tilman said. "Butter, let's go back up to the change station and see if we can use a couple of horses to get to the fort. I'm sure Law will send them back on their next run in this direction."

The station manager proved agreeable, and they were soon on the way by horse. It felt good to them to be back in the saddle again, even if they had to be light McClellan saddles. Sunset found Butter and Tilman on the outskirts of the town of Fort Davis as a bugle sounded the evening recall from the fort, the sound echoing over the quiet of the prairie and soon answered by howling dogs. Water trickled down the sides of the dirt road running through man-made *acequias,* the irrigation ditches that criss-crossed farm plots around the town. A line of massive cottonwoods, a hundred years old or more, separated the town from the fort. The rays of the afternoon sun made the cottonwoods glow a brilliant yellow, brighter than gold leaf.

"I ain't never seen nothing like it in all my born days!" Butter stopped his horse and removed his hat to study the leaves. "I thought the sound of aspen when the wind whistled through 'em was something, but this"—he paused—"this is sheer poetry."

Tilman laughed. "Butter, you old rascal. You sound like you should be writing verse instead of hunting Apaches."

"Don't let my fancy manners fool you, Tilman my

boy." Butter placed his worn hat firmly on his head. "I'm mean as they come."

They continued on toward Fort Davis. Both men knew the trees were nothing more than a last excuse to stop, a final moment of peace and calm before they faced the trouble they'd come so far to meet.

Chapter Twelve

Fort Davis, an open post, offered no defensive walls around the fort. It sat astride the El Paso to San Antonio road at the mouth of a canyon cut through high bluffs to the north. Sentries were placed to observe the approaches to the fort.

Challenged and halted by a roadside sentry—a young black soldier armed with a Springfield carbine—at what appeared to be the post boundary, Tilman gave his name. "Where can I find Captain Law?"

"I'll get somebody to help you," the sentry said. He turned and bawled, "Corporal of the guard, post number one!"

The call was echoed by another sentry farther away. Hardly a minute passed before a mounted soldier reined his horse onto the road and trotted to Tilman and Butter. After a brief explanation, they followed the corporal to the dismount point by the post headquarters at the east end of the parade ground. The parade, a large well-kept open field, covered a rectangle of about five acres with a flag pole in the center; it was bordered on one side by four large whitewashed barracks buildings and across the parade stood a line of twelve handsome stone houses. A small group of black soldiers sat in the shaded porch of one of the barracks buildings cleaning rifles.

"Cap'n Law's in there," the soldier said, as he turned to ride away.

"Well, I'll just be double . . ." Butter's voice trailed off at the sight of black men in Army uniforms coming and going. "I figgered that guard was the only one, but all these soldiers here is darkys," Butter said in wonder.

"Ain't darkys. They're Buffalo Soldiers," a man said, and Tilman looked as a huge, black man stood at the entrance to the post headquarters, the whites of his eyes bloodshot and watery. The man would stand probably six-foot-six, but with boots and hat he was close to seven-feet tall.

"I see you're still above ground, Smith," Tilman said.

"I heard you was coming," the man squinted at Tilman in the bright sunlight. "Might've known. I got a scar giving me fits this morning." He rubbed the back of his head as he spoke.

"Butter, this is Gus Smith. He's a civilian scout for the Army, and a fair tracker. I gave him that scar."

"Howdy." Butter reached out and shook the man's hand. "Are there more like you back home?"

"Nope. They're all dead as far as I know." Turning to Tilman, the man continued. "I owe you one back. Good thing you're here for Captain Law, else you'n me'd hafta settle this right here and now. Cap'n Law, he's a good man. That daughter means the world to him."

Smith walked down the steps and around Tilman's horse, swung onto his own mount and headed east off the post.

"Call me nosey, but what'd I miss here, Tilman?"

"A few years back Smith worked at Fort McKavett where I was. He got drunk out in Hogtown across the San Saba River from the post. I rode in with a deserter I'd picked up, and it seemed that bad blood flowed between Gus and that deserter. Gus saw us, and went after him. I tried to stop Gus. He always carried a knife in his boot and so he went after the prisoner with it. I clubbed Smith with my pistol, cut his head pretty bad when I hit him, but not before he cut up the prisoner so bad the man died a few days later."

The two men dismounted as John Law came out of his office.

"Tilman, I thought that was you!" Law shook hands with Tilman, looking at Butter.

"It's been a while." Tilman read the worry lines etched into his friend's face. "We'll do all we can to help, John. Now, before we tell any tall tales we'll regret, I've brought some of the best help Colorado has to offer. I'd like you to meet my good friend Butter Pegram. We'll do our best to bring those girls home to you. I give you my word."

Chapter Thirteen

In his "headquarters," a cave in the steep, high walls of Santa Elena Canyon locally known as Smugglers Cave, Chuy Ayala poured himself another drink of tequila. "Guns," he mumbled aloud, "I need guns." *La revolucion*, Chuy thought, *is not going well*. For years the government in Mexico City had ignored the pleas from the people who lived in the far north where the state of Chihuahua bordered on the United States, and were desperately crying for help in fending off frequent raids by both Comanche and Apache Indians and border bandits. Indians and bandits crossed the Rio Bravo at will to steal cattle and horses, kidnap women and children, pillage and kill Mexican farmers struggling to exist in the rugged country of the north. At other times they came to sell or trade captives and goods stolen in Texas. Who could know their minds?

Chuy himself had suffered at their brutal hands— when he was sixteen years old his family's *rancho* had been attacked and the house burned with the family trapped inside. Chuy alone had managed to escape, but his face was permanently disfigured by the flames. He fought against the raiders and soon his army would rid the land of those Apaches. Then he would lead his men against the governor. Known as El Chamuscado, the Scorched One, his was a name to be feared.

Chuy fought the governor of Chihuahua because he believed the man to be weak. Why else would he fail to forcefully demand help from the *federales*? And so, at the age of twenty-five, Chuy decided to take matters into his own hands, for surely he could do better for the people, and for Chuy Ayala. He gathered an oddly mixed band of battle-hardened men who had lost their homes and families to the Indians. The men were idealists, border-jumping toughs, and half-breeds joined together to form a small army, which he scattered in small bands across northern Chihuahua.

On one of his raids south of the border Chuy found a small printing press and, until his printer deserted, delighted in publishing an occasional newspaper expounding on the virtues of Chuy and of his cause. When he became too much of a thorn in the side of the authorities, the Mexican Army would ride after him and Chuy would shift to the American side of the border to operate. When he raided in Texas the Americans would tolerate him until too many cattle and horses disappeared from their ranches, and then the U.S. Cavalry would come and push Chuy back into Mexico.

Chuy needed modern guns to stand up against the small forces the governor sometimes sent to pursue him; however, they were armed with repeating rifles bought from *norteamericanos*. Success for Chuy depended on getting more and better guns. He had heard that in Texas the *soldados* at Fort Davis had guns that would shoot hundreds of bullets a minute. Luis said they were called Gatling guns, and if only he could get one he was certain his forces would be victorious against the governor, the Indians, anyone. But how could he get one of those? Buy it? Steal it? Who knew?

His goal was nothing less than bringing about the secession of the state of Chihuahua from Mexico. When that happened he would install himself as the leader of a newly independent state across the river from Texas. Fortunately for Chuy his uprising coincided with the Yaqui and Mayan uprising which began in 1875 in Sonora. Their early successes caused the government to concentrate the Army against them rather than against Chuy. However, when the situation in Sonora became manageable, then Chuy would receive the full attention of the federal government. The fact that the Army of Chihuahua was heavily engaged against Apache raiders from San Carlos in Arizona and *rancherias* in New Mexico territory freed Chuy from immediate pursuit.

In Lajitas, the *Tejano* town just across the river, his man Luis Valenzuela kept an eye out for any opportunity to obtain the guns and supplies Chuy's army needed so badly. Luis had reported that he might be able to pay one of the soldiers at the fort to get some of their guns. After all, the soldier, who had a thirst for tequila and women almost as powerful as his hate for the officers at the fort, had sold his own sidearm to Luis so he could buy a bottle. The gun was a magnificent single-action Army Colt .45, almost new, which Chuy now proudly wore. He must see Luis, have him talk to his *Sargento* Lusk, and demand one of the Gatling guns.

He would send Comes From War to find Luis. Comes From War was a man of uncertain loyalties, a mixed blood of many races who joined Chuy's forces after being chased across the border by the *gringos* last year. He was a good fighter, but often drank too much, and he was a mean drunk. But then, so were many of his *revolucionarios*.

Comes From War rode into Lajitas and left his horse at the hitching post by an old cantina frequented by Luis Valenzuela. Thick adobe-brick walls kept the temperature in the dark interior comfortable year around. Out of habit the mixed blood stepped through the door, moved to his right and immediately pressed his back to the wall until his eyes adjusted from the bright sunlight outside. He studied the faces of the men who turned to see who had entered before they returned to drink and cards. Luis, a man careful in his dress and grooming, was there. He wore an embroidered short leather *vaquero* jacket over a clean white linen shirt. His carefully tailored black woolen pants had three rows of silver buttons lining the outside seams, and the flared bottoms were hand-embroidered. Luis was proud of his fine black leather boots and large-roweled polished silver spurs. A black sombrero hung on his back. Luis sat at a long table across from two Apaches. A half empty tequila bottle and several shot glasses separated the men. All three smoked long, thin cigars. In the shadows at the back of the cantina a young white woman with frightened eyes sat beside a sleeping white girl. They were bound with rawhide strips. Comes From War nodded to Luis, and strode to the bar. He ordered tequila and stood impassive, listening, his drink untouched. Comes From War studied the woman when no one else was looking. He noticed that the woman had hair like the fine strands on maize when the corn ripened in the field. It was so light it appeared as white. She was dirty from riding but she was still a woman of fire. She would be a good woman for him, one to warm his blankets in winter. Comes From War knew he could wait. If Luis bought the women and took them to Chuy's camp then he would find an opportunity to be alone with the woman. He intended to take it!

A neatly trimmed mustache framed his broad smile as Luis spoke with Joseph Half Man, who translated for the other Indian. "I am a man who deals in guns, cigars, horses, many things needed by strong men," he explained. "White women can be trouble, and they attract attention when I do not care for it."

Joseph Half Man translated for Whips His Horse, who only nodded. Joseph Half Man said to Luis, "The woman works at the white man's fort. She is much woman for any man. The girl is the daughter of a chief at the fort. We no touch. She is worth much whiskey, many horses."

"Perhaps," Luis said, concealing his new and sudden interest in the two white captives the men wanted to sell. "Let us drink and consider this thing." As he spoke, Luis idly toyed with three walnut shells and a pea. With half-closed, sleepy eyes he seemed bored, uninterested, but his mind raced. The daughter of an American officer might be traded for something valuable, and El Chamuscado must know of this.

Whips His Horse pointed at one of the shells. Luis lifted the shell to reveal the pea. "Your eyes are very sharp, *amigo*." He smiled. "Again?"

Maddie watched the exchange between the Indians and the well-dressed man. The man they called Luis was what she had heard the ladies at the fort call "a dandy." Lomida stirred and Maddie knew she only pretended to sleep so she poked her in the side. "Lomida, I think the man who is so dressed up must have a closet filled with clothes." It was an attempt to distract, to amuse the girl in a place where nothing was amusing.

Lomida pulled herself up to sit by Maddie and looked at Luis even though the rawhide rope slowed her movement as she tried to sit up. "Look at the embroidery on his vest. He reminds me of a peacock." Lomida closed her eyes and pictured Luis strutting around the room. "I don't see any tail feathers though, Miss Maddie."

"*Basta*. Enough. No talk." Joseph Half Man turned to toss an empty bottle in their direction. It landed harmlessly to the side of Maddie but she knew he was drinking heavily so she had better be quiet. At least they could listen and maybe even learn their fate in the game unfolding before them. Maddie whispered, "Lomida, pay close attention to what they say. I think our lives are involved in this game."

Lomida nodded agreement, once again closing her eyes but listening intently.

Soon the game became more serious. The shells seemed to be a favorite with Luis, and even Maddie could see by the cunning look in his eyes that he was very good at the game.

"Five will get you ten," Luis said smoothly moving

the shells around the table, "and ten will get you twenty. What is hidden under my little 'umbrellas?' See, it's very easy. Make your choice, and if you are right you win." He paused. "But I tell you now odds are two to your one that you will not beat Luis."

Comes From War watched intently when one of the two men who had been drinking at a table near the bar looked at Maddie, spoke to his friend, and laughed and then pushed his chair back. He was unwashed. He wore high-topped moccasins, filthy pants, and a greasy buckskin shirt, but his pistol and knife were well cared for; a big man, his once massive chest had become a big potbelly, muscle gone to fat, and he lumbered to Maddie and fell beside her on the floor. Maddie recoiled in fear as the man stretched one arm about her shoulders, pulled her to him and tried to kiss her. Beard stubble scratched her face, and breath foul with drink, and rotten, blackened teeth caused her to gag. He let go, leaned back and drank again from his bottle; he called for his friend.

"Come here. Hold this 'un down for me."

Wordlessly, without losing his concentration on the game, Luis glanced at Comes From War and nodded his head. Silently, as deadly as a springing panther, Comes From War crossed the room, and stood over the big man. Comes From War, with one hand resting on the knife in his belt, looked down at the big man and kicked his foot saying, "You, go."

"Just who in . . ." When he looked into Comes From War's flat, expressionless eyes he saw imminent death—his own. Comes From War curled his hand around the knife, made as if to draw it. The man measured his chances at getting his gun out, but whiskey courage fled, leaving the big man weak and uncertain.

"No, you don' want to do that," came Luis' calm, measured voice.

Maddie, tearing her eyes from the drama before her, looked first at Luis and then at the big man's friend. The other one had started to rise to help his friend, a gun partly drawn but not yet clear of its holster. The man stood unmoving, half out of his chair. Maddie looked again at Luis, and this time she saw a big silver pistol in his hand, the barrel pointed directly and unwaveringly at the man's middle. Luis squeezed the trigger until the hammer of the double action pistol was at full cock. The slightest additional pressure of his finger would hurl a man into eternity.

Lomida's eyes were closed; she held her breath in fear.

Comes From War took the now defeated man by his collar, dragged him to his feet and pushed him across the room to his friend at the table.

"You go, now. Take him."

Maddie tasted bile rising in her throat and choked it back. A brutal man had just backed down beside her simply because he looked into the Indian's eyes. Who were these people who held her captive? A man cowed, backing down in the blink of an eye. What kind of cruelty was inside that Indian? What was he truly capable of doing? The two white men left, reminding Maddie of whipped dogs slinking away into the night.

The shells seemed to favor the Apaches, with Luis losing money to them, only now and again winning a little of it back. Another bottle was ordered. "Let us up the stakes, my friends." Luis placed his fine spurs on the table, and his pistol, an engraved nickel-plated Russian .44 with ivory grips. The betting continued. By the time the second bottle was empty, the two Apaches were glassy-eyed and sat tottering, semi-conscious in their seats. In the end Luis had won the captives, and he still wore his spurs and the engraved .44, and oddly, he did not appear the least bit drunk. By some amazing sleight of hand he appeared to have matched the Indians drink for drink yet he had not. Maddie wondered about the strange man who now controlled her destiny.

Luis gathered up his belongings. He looked appraisingly at Maddie, then back at the Indians. Making a dusting motion with his hands, Luis said, "*Hecho,*" signifying that the deal, his winning of the captives, was done.

As the sun disappeared below the western horizon, Luis guided his horse along the darkening trail through Santa Elena Canyon. The canyon, perhaps five miles downriver from Lajitas, narrowed as the trail followed alongside the river. In the close, still air the hollow clatter of the horses' hoofs on stones and the horses' snorting echoed through the early evening. Maddie and Lomida rode on burros close behind Luis, while behind them rode Comes From War. His blood ran hot as he watched Maddie with hungry, wolfish eyes.

The idea came to Luis as he rode in silence. He must propose a trade, a ransom to the girl's father at the fort: Her life for a Gatling gun. Chuy would be pleased, and much good would come to Luis for his work.

Chapter Fourteen

The patrol's big, grain-fed cavalry mounts were broken down for they had been too long on the trail. A common saying in the West held that a cavalryman would ride a horse into the ground after twenty miles; a cowboy could get on that same horse and get another ten miles out of him, and a Mexican could take that horse and get yet another twenty miles before abandoning him to a Comanche, who would ride that horse fifty miles further and then eat him.

Sol Burney could not close the gap on the Indians, and because he arrived at Lajitas just at dusk, he lost the trail in a confusion of tracks. He halted his patrol, dismounted to stretch and to study the town, such as it was. There were a few adobe *jacales,* mud and stick huts thrown together for a one or two-room dwelling. Several buildings made of stacked stones with thick reeds for a roof, a store of the same materials, a corral, and several cantinas faced a single dusty, rutted street. On the other side of the village he saw a church steeple with a broken cross.

"I've been here before, lieutenant," Sergeant Leoni said. "I know a man we can trust. Why don't we detail Corporal Jefferson to take the men and wait at that corral, cool the horses and water them while you and I go look around?"

An old man sat outside one of the *jacales* which offered a good view of the main street of the town. Leoni hailed the man, *"Como es usted, viejo?"*

"Hola, sargento. Come, sit and my old woman will bring us cool water to drink."

"Mil gracias. But today we sit too much and we must stand for a while."

The old man laughed, and called his wife to bring the *olla* and some cups.

A woman wrinkled by many years spent working under the hot sun, placed a large clay jug filled with water next to the men. She smiled, revealing several missing teeth, and disappeared as quietly as she had come.

"Sometimes, I think water is better than tequila," Leoni joked with the old man. "Sometimes." They all laughed and settled down to business.

Burney was introduced, watched, and learned. Leoni placed a bag of tobacco and cigarette papers on the table by the *olla,* and from an inside pocket of his jacket came a small, silver flask that he opened and passed around. The old man raised the flask, murmured *"Salud,"* took a drink and then rolled a cigarette. Burney started to speak then stopped as he saw Leoni motion for him to be still. The art of conversation in this small town was a delicate dance. Burney tried to roll a cigarette and quickly gave up as the tobacco fell out, so he settled for a small swig from the flask. "The *teniente,* he is young, *mi amigo.* But, he learns. He will do."

The three men sat in the fading sunlight, each savoring a quiet moment in a troubled time. Finally, the old man asked, "Do you come for the white women who came with *los Indios*?"

"*Sí.*"

"I have not seen them myself, but I am told that a man, Luis Valenzuela, now owns them. He has taken them this very day to the Santa Elena Canyon, across the border and into Mexico. I do not know where he will go, but white women who are taken across the border do not return. They are lost." With that he softly clapped his hands once, more a brushing of the hands, to indicate the finality of his words.

"What do we do now, lieutenant?" Leoni asked as they returned to the corral where the men waited.

"I want to go after them, but . . ."

Leoni waited for Burney to finish what he started to say.

"That's an international border. Even in this God-forsaken place, it's still the border between two countries. As an officer I can't lead armed troops across it without orders."

"You came here without orders," Leoni pointed out.

Burney paused, unsure of what to do. What did they say about this sort of thing in his military law classes at the Point? He couldn't remember. He would have to decide for himself. "We'll rest tonight. Post a guard. We'll head back to the fort at first light."

Meanwhile, Luis and his captives entered Chuy's camp at dusk. Chuy, as usual, had chosen well. The steep walls of the canyon made Chuy's camp an excellent place to hide in safety from unwanted intruders. His camp was accessible by only the one path along the river and that path could be watched and easily covered by rifle fire from above. Even better, it was on the Mexican side and Luis and Chuy both knew that made it immune from attack by the *norteamericanos*. The large opening of a natural cave carved by waters seeping through the earth over tens of thousands of years offered a perfect setting for Chuy's camp. More recently, the river had cut a steep-walled canyon over four-hundred-feet deep as the mesa thrust upward along a fault line to reveal the cave. Before men came the cave served as a refuge for many animals whose bones could yet be found in the cool, deep recesses where few dared to venture. Pure, fresh water bubbled from springs in the cave, and the river provided driftwood for fires. However, the men who used the cave had no eye for its natural beauty. They cared only for its remoteness, its defensibility. Besides, who would bother with a few local smugglers? They were not worth any effort to find and evict.

The girls were tired and dirty and they were hungry. They didn't look like much of a catch for anybody, but Luis knew differently and he had only to convince Chuy.

"Luis!" Chuy joined the group as the girls slid off the burros. "What have you brought me?" Chuy circled the girls as Luis gave a surly Comes From War orders to take care of the animals.

"The woman is not too bad if we clean her up, but look." Luis lifted the side of Lomida's skirt displaying her crippled leg, enjoying her discomfort as she saw Chuy's burned face and tried not to grimace.

"What's the matter, little one? Does my face frighten you?" He jeered. "Maybe your twisted leg bothers me."

He turned to Luis, "Explain to me. I sent you to find out about guns, not women captives."

"*Si, esta claro.* Sure. But." Luis pulled Chuy to the side of the enclosure, leaving Maddie and Lomida standing alone in the growing darkness, not sure what to do but realizing that to do nothing was best. Luis pointed to Lomida. "I know the little one is not so good, but her father is one of the officers at the fort. The pretty one is the schoolteacher. We can sell her or trade her back, but the little one should be worth a Gatling gun." Luis, pleased with himself, turned and looked at Chuy. "What do you think?"

Chuy thought about the change of plans, walked once more around the girls, and returned to Luis' side. It made sense, and if such a ransom could be made—a Gatling gun for the daughter of a soldier—he could get what he wanted.

"A plan that is worthy of me, Luis. You have done well. We will have our gun. White men are foolish about children." He paused as they made their way to a crude bar at the opening to the cave. "And, if the *gringos* refuse, well, when I am finished with the woman she will still be worth much in trade in Mexico City. Even the girl is of some value. Old men desire youth, even with imperfections." He stared at Lomida as she stood by the evening fire. "And such hair. Look at it in the firelight. I have never seen hair that color. Yes, Luis, you have done well."

Several hours later Luis and Chuy, full from a meal of cabrito, frijoles, tortillas and tequila, sat and finalized their plans for the ransom. Lomida and Maddie had been placed in one of the crude huts with a guard placed at the door with orders to shoot anyone who tried to bother them; Chuy knew his men. A stoic Comes From War watched from a distance and then went to his blankets. He could wait for the right time. He was a patient man.

"Luis, *mi hermano.* Tomorrow I want you to ride to the fort and present our demands to the man in charge. One Gatling gun for the girl, and five thousand bullets for the woman. It is fair, their lives for those things. If the man chooses not to comply they will be sold in Mexico City. Either way we win."

"*Mi Jefe,* what do I say when they ask the time? Two weeks? Three?"

Chuy, who considered himself a spiritual man, thought and said, "*La Posada* goes until the day of Christmas so we will give them the thirty days until that time. This way they will know we are soldiers fighting for a cause, just as they are, and men of honor, not criminals. Our cause is to take this land from those unworthy of it, those who would rule it from afar." Chuy patted his holstered pistol as he drew himself up to his full five-foot-six. "We need their gun to help us fight. We are giving them time to make the arrangements and bring the gun to us."

Luis agreed. It seemed a long time to him, but he knew Chuy's violent temper when anyone dared to disagree with him, and so Luis said nothing. Chuy suddenly drew his knife, made his way to the hut where the girls were sleeping, motioned for the guard to move aside and entered the room. A sudden cry was heard and Chuy came back out carrying something in his hands. He handed Luis the two objects. "Take these with you and the soldiers will know we mean business."

In his hands Luis held two locks of hair, one silver blond and the other dark red.

Chapter Fifteen

Dear Catherine,

In good health I take pen in hand this fine clear morning and hope that my letter will find you are well. Butter and I arrived at Fort Davis several days ago and we are sure glad to be done riding for a day or so. An Army lieutenant brought in a patrol last night. The soldiers tracked the Apaches to Lajitas, a village on the Mexican border, a hard day's ride south of Fort Davis. The girls were lost in a gambling game to a rascal named Luis Valenzuela. At least we know Lomida was alive and well at that time. They say this Valenzuela is the right hand man of a fellow named Chuy Ayala. Chuy is a smuggler and a thief with his own band of renegades.

The soldiers quit the chase because Luis took the girls across the border and so now Butter and I come into play as we are not bound by the Army's rules. John is worried sick about the girls as he has heard nothing new. Perhaps we'll learn more today.

There is talk here about how John ought to leave everything and go get Lomida and the teacher. Those that say that don't know the kind of man John is. John swore an oath and he is a man of honor. He is in charge of the fort while Colonel Grierson is out with his patrol. Word has come to John that one of the women here is very harsh in judging him. She is the quartermaster's wife, a bitter woman.

I am glad that Butter is here with me. He is a comfort with his good humor and common sense.

How is James? Hope he hasn't had any fights since I left. I have been gone only a few days but it seems like a lot more. I also find that I want to share this trip with you. Butter and I saw huge cottonwoods along Limpia Creek and they were like gold. I also thought of you in Santa Fe on our trip. You would have liked the sidewalk vendors and the jewelry.

We are meeting with John shortly to decide our strategy and I will write again later.

Hoping you will write to me,
Tilman Wagner
PS My ribs are doing much better. They hurt some but are almost well

With a china mug of steaming black coffee in his hand, Tilman stood hatless in the crisp early morning air under a deep, cloudless blue sky. The smell of freshly baking bread came to Tilman from the post bakery over by the San Antonio-El Paso road. His joints ached, but not as bad as they had on those cold Colorado mornings. He and Butter were assigned rooms in a large, two-story adobe house used by bachelor officers at the post, all of whom were now in the field with the regiment. At a table on the porch of the quarters someone, probably John's orderly, had left a pot of coffee and two mugs just after reveille sounded. There was also a still-warm loaf of fresh bread, some sliced cheese, and slabs of fried bacon under a cloth. It was good chuck, especially since Tilman didn't have to rustle it up himself.

Activity at the far end of the parade field caught Tilman's eye. A lone soldier rode past the enlisted men's barracks at full gallop and pulled to a halt in front of the post headquarters; the rider hit the ground running and disappeared into the building on the other side of the post chapel from where Tilman stood. Such early morning excitement struck Tilman as being out of the ordinary. Most of the soldiers were away in the field and the place seemed pretty quiet.

On impulse Tilman put down his mug and went back into his room to grab his hat. He awakened Butter. "I'm going to John's quarters to see what is going on, Butter. Get dressed and meet me there." Butter nodded sleepily as Tilman left, calling over his shoulder, "Chuck's on the porch, and coffee." A bugler stepped from the headquarters building and sounded "Officers' Call." As with every bugle call, the post dogs howled.

Tilman got to Law's quarters, the closest house on Officers' Row and only a few yards distant, as John came out the front door in his shirtsleeves. "Morning, John. Maybe there's news about the girls." John took the napkin he was wiping his hands with from breakfast and handed it to his orderly, who went back into the house.

As they spoke, First Sergeant Duncannon hurried across the parade grounds. He saluted John. "Morning, sir."

"What's going on?"

"Chuy Ayala's men are here under a white flag; one of them is Luis Valenzuela. Sergeant Durbin said they want to talk, sir. He sent them to the post trader's store to wait for you."

Sergeant Durbin came from the stables leading three saddled horses and halted on the street. Along Officers' Row women and children stood on porches or peered out windows behind drawn back curtains, curiously watching the unfolding drama. The orderly held John's coat. "Side arm, sir?"

"No." To Duncannon he said, "They're here to parley, but fall out the guard relief and surround the trader's just to keep 'em honest." John motioned for Tilman to follow. "Let's go." The men started for the store.

Butter, ever mindful of his stomach had paused for a quick breakfast and hurried along behind them afoot, strapping on a belted pistol as he came. Word spread quickly on the small post. All pretense at activity had stopped as the women in front of their houses anxiously watched Tilman, John, and the others as they headed out of the housing area.

Inside the post trader's, it was quiet but for the ticking of a clock on the fireplace mantel. The storekeeper stood behind the bar and nervously polished glasses as two well-armed Mexicans, one a well-dressed dandy of a man while the other, clearly a *pistolero*, sat at a table. Their white flag leaned against the wall by the door. Both men faced the door, as alert and wary as caged lions. Sounds of horses and men brought the store-keeper to the front of the building and when he saw Captain Law he quietly disappeared into the back room.

Luis, concealing his surprise that only one of the *gringos*, the old one, wore a pistol, stood as the men entered. Luis spoke first in an assured manner. *"Buenos dias, senores."* With a practiced move he smoothed the end of his glistening mustache with the knuckle of his right index finger, plainly enjoying his control of the situation. "Please, let us be seated."

Sergeant Duncannon came in, nodded to Law to indicate that guards now surrounded the building, and stood guard by the door. John Law fought to control his anger. He knew the Mexican had come because of the girls, and he had to hear the man out if there was even a possibility of ever seeing Lomida and Maddie alive. "Why are you men here? It is early in the day for a social call."

Luis acknowledged John but looked at Tilman and Butter. "Who are these men, *Capitan*? I do not know them from my earlier visits to this fort."

"I'm Wagner and he's Pegram. We're friends of Captain Law. Just happened to be in town, you might say." Tilman looked at Luis and held his gaze until Luis blinked and turned to John.

"Good. A man should have friends." Luis made a note to find out about the two men and continued. "Captain Law, into my *jefe*'s care have come two young women who may be known to you. They were won in a game of chance in Lajitas some days ago. I assure you they are safe for now. How happy it is for us when we find the one is your daughter and the other a schoolteacher."

John's face did not reflect the flood of relief he felt in hearing that Lomida and Miss Brown were alive, if not safe.

Luis continued. "What a tragic occurrence if they were to end up lost in Mexico City or met with a bad end someplace out in the desert. Is that not true?"

"Your point, *senor* . . . uh . . ."

"Valenzuela, Luis Valenzuela, at your orders."

It was needless to lose his temper. John knew men like this and he was aware they enjoyed their moments of glory. Luis held the high card for now and he knew it. John would bide his time. Lomida's and Maddie's future rested in his hands.

"My point is very simple, *senor*. We have something you want, and you have something we want. Chuy Ayala wants a thing you have in the fort and in exchange he will gladly return your daughter and the other woman safely back to you. Should you choose to refuse this thing the young women will be sold. They will bring a lot of money so he must have something of great value."

John Law listened carefully. What did this man want? "Speak up, man. What do we have? We are a small fort. We have very little money."

"No, *Capitan*. You misunderstand. From you we don' want money. We want one of your guns. I believe it is called a Gatling?" Luis looked at their surprised faces and smiled. "Surely you would know that we are aware of such guns. *Mi jefe* will use it to fight for his cause. He is meant to be a great leader and he can do so much better with one of the fast firing Gatling guns. Would you not agree?"

"You are surrounded, Valenzuela. How would it be if we trade your life for the girls?"

"It would not happen, *Capitan*. If I fail to return, Chuy will get the money but you will not get the girls."

"I must think about what you say," John said.

"Very well." Luis stood, motioned to the man with him to get the white flag and started out the door. "*Mi jefe*, because he is *religioso,* will be celebrating the Posada until the day of Christmas. You have until that time to bring the gun. I will be in Lajitas and we will arrange the trade. Your daughter for the gun, and for the other woman, five thousand cartridges. If, *capitan*"— Luis hesitated, never taking his eyes off John—"if by Christmas Eve we do not have the gun, the girls will be separated and sold in Mexico City." Luis nodded to Tilman and then to Butter. "*Adios, amigos.*" Motioning, he and the other man turned and left.

Chapter Sixteen

A Gatling gun? There was no way John could give away a Gatling gun. Tilman studied John. Hard choices. "John, are you . . ."

"Tilman, we have to figure out a way to make these bandits think we're going along with them. They could move Lomida and Maddie someplace we can never get to them. I've heard of this Chuy Ayala. He's called El Chamuscado because one side of his face is badly burned from when he was a child. Lately he has stayed on the Mexican side of the border. But, he's played the devil now."

Later, in his office, John explained to Tilman and Butter. "Lieutenant Burney trailed the Indians to Lajitas, and then stopped—they were tired, their horses were worn out, and his was a small patrol. Burney's only been in the West a few weeks. I'd sent him out to learn the lay of the land, not to fight." John blamed himself. "I should have made his orders more general, but I suppose because he's so green I tied his hands. The lad knew he couldn't *legally* cross the border. A more experienced officer, in hot pursuit of hostiles with white captives, would have found a way to get the job done. I did, when I was at Fort Clark, but I was a veteran, and I'd been around the Army a lot longer than he has. I was going to accomplish my mission, no matter what. Well, I figure the young officer will learn, if he lives long enough."

"What's done is done," Butter offered, "an' we'll just have go on down there an' find 'em."

"But to give the Devil his due," Tilman said, "that boy took a risk when he left El Muerto and trailed them to the south. He changed his orders without authority, and could be court-martialed for that. He just needs seasoning, to know just how far he *can* go in a situation like that."

"If only Colonel Grierson was here, I could come with you. I know there has been talk." John wearily smiled. "Grierson is after Lone Wolf's Apaches. You've heard of him? Some call him Chief Victorio, and he raids both sides of the border. Grierson has no choice but to continue until they have gotten this renegade."

John pulled his chair closer and spoke quietly. "I got news a couple of days ago that Lone Wolf and his warriors ambushed and killed fifteen Mexican citizens who were looking for cattle thieves. The victims were from a little village across the border in the Candelaria Mountains. Then, as if that wasn't enough, ten or eleven more people were killed hunting for the first group of men. The Mexican government has telegraphed us that they are trying to drive the Apaches back into Texas. So, Grierson is keeping the 10th

Cavalry out to head off Lone Wolf if he comes back."
John paused. "It's a long border. There are a lot of
places a man can go if he doesn't want to be found. And
old Lone Wolf is one of the best at evading us."

"So you had better stay put," Butter surmised. "We
can get your little girl, John. Let's just figure out the
particulars." Butter spoke calmly and with confidence,
more confidence than Tilman felt. The odds were all
against rescuing the girls.

"Here's what I think," John said. "I'll give you one
Gatling, with its ammunition limber—I'll worry about
consequences later. I'd rather ask for forgiveness than
ask permission. You can have Lieutenant Burney and
Sergeant Leoni and two troopers. That's all I can spare.
We have one civilian scout who knows that country and
might help— Smith. You've met him, I believe."

"I have."

"The gun's bait."

"So, what's your plan?"

"Tilman, I don't have one."

"What?"

"You'll have to figure the best thing to do when you
get there. You've got to get Lomida back. Miss Brown
too. I hope you can do that and keep the gun out of
Ayala's hands. If you lose that gun, I'll be court-
martialed and disgraced."

"Your plan is for me to make up my plan when I get
there?"

"You'll be the best judge of the situation as you see
it. It's up to you."

"Great God!" Tilman exclaimed. "You don't ask
much of a man!"

"I don't have any choice, do I?"

After a long silence, John asked, "Then you'll do it?"

"I got no choice."

"Well," Butter said, "reckon our wills best be up to date."

The storm howled in on a cold dusty wind, a classic Texas norther that drove men indoors and sent the post's dogs scrambling for shelter while women ran to gather drying laundry off the lines and to call in the little ones from play. A quick flash of lightning followed by a sharp crack of thunder accompanied a downpour of much needed rain and beat on the roof of the headquarters building. "What now?" Butter looked at the ceiling and put a used spittoon under a steady drip from the roof. "I thought this country was supposed to be drier than my grandpappy's scalp."

"Usually is this time of year." John walked over to the door and looked out. Sheets of rain cut his vision of the mountains. "I sent Smith to follow Luis from a distance, but with this deluge his tracks will be gone already."

Law gave Burney written orders to draw supplies and marching rations for eight days and to have his men ready to move out in two days with the gun and a fully stocked ammunition limber. To Tilman he said, "The gun you're taking is one that the Army bought in 1866, and modified to .45 caliber. It's due to be shipped off to the ordnance depot at Jefferson Barracks and cut up for scrap. It only works some of the time. It's worn, and the ammunition feed magazines don't fit tightly, and you get stoppages from that. Mostly it just jams after the barrels get hot."

"You're telling me if we get in a tight spot and have to shoot our way out, that gun is next to worthless?"

"Well, Duncannon will put a powder charge in the ammunition limber chest cut with a ten-second fuse. If you have to you can blow up the gun and the ammunition."

Smith came stomping into the headquarters, pulled off a dripping rain slicker and reported just what John had feared. The rain had wiped out all of Luis' tracks and he had disappeared in the storm as quietly as he had come. All that remained was the white flag on a stick he found on the prairie about five miles south of the town of Fort Davis. It was stuck in a cactus. Plainly Luis expected to be followed.

"But Captain"—Augustus Smith was clearly uncomfortable with what he was carrying—"this was on the flag pole." Smith handed a small bag to John and waited while he opened the bag. Inside were two pieces of hair, one silver-blond and the other a dark red.

The room was silent as the seriousness of the situation stopped conversation.

Tilman finally broke the quiet as he looked at Butter. "Shouldn't we learn how to use that fancy gun?"

"Sure. I've heard of them things but never seen one."

John stood. "After the rain lets up. I'll have the men drag that monster out to the firing range first thing tomorrow."

Morning came in cold with gray clouds hanging low and threatening, ominous. Tilman and Butter were restless, and not just because the weather changed. While waiting for the Gatling demonstration, they decided to ride into Fort Davis and look around. Passing near the town square Butter sniffed appreciatively as the aroma of fresh cinnamon rolls wafted across the street.

"Mercy! Where do you suppose that heavenly smell's coming from?"

"Butter. If you don't beat all." Tilman pointed in the direction of the small hotel and general store at the corner across from the cut-stone courthouse. The town had grown up out of a need for civilian workers at the fort and to support a growing ranch population in the surrounding hills. There existed a sense of settling down here as Tilman and Butter noticed children playing in front of small homes down side streets. The main street offered a place to board, a restaurant, a butcher shop and the general mercantile store, and of course there were several saloons. A lawyer hung his shingle outside a small office. There were stables with a barn and hayloft, a stage station and a smithy. All in all it was a prosperous, thriving community.

"Here's where it's coming from." Butter stopped his horse and dismounted, led by his nose into the general store. Tilman stopped, knowing that until Butter got his fill of whatever it was he was after, Tilman might as well settle down. They went into the store to look around. The owner appeared to be busy filling an order from a woman who carried a fussy baby on one arm. The store shelves were amply stocked with canned goods, tables held ready-made work clothes, and there were barrels of pickles, a strong-smelling cheese, sacks of coffee and boxes of tea. There was a wood-burning stove in the middle of the store, two straight-backed wooden chairs and a spittoon. By the front window, bolts of cloth and sewing needs and ladies' ready-made clothing were on display.

Off to the side was a small room that obviously

served as a small bakery. "Ain't that where that heavenly smell is a-comin' from?" Butter became animated with anticipation. He looked at the counter but there were no baked goods there. "I could smell it . . . I swear I could."

"This what you're talking about?"

Butter stopped. He turned and stared, not at the piping hot cinnamon rolls, but at the tall goddess bearing a tray of thick, white-topped rolls. Blond tendrils of hair escaped the tidy bun and large blue eyes twinkled as Butter looked up, yes, looked up. The woman was at least half a foot taller than him and would ever be one to stand out in a crowd. Butter was struck almost dumb, as if by lightning.

Tilman watched his friend from the door. He had never known Butter to lack for words.

"I asked you if you want a cinnamon roll."

"Uh. Excuse me, ma'am." Butter removed his hat, holding it with both hands to his chest. "I reckon I'm just bowled over by that aroma." Butter looked toward the back room. "Your husband must be a mighty lucky man if you're the baker."

"Miss Neala Barry's my name. There ain't no husband. Not that there haven't been offers mind you. I just ain't been interested. I live with my brother James. We have a spread out from town."

Butter pointed to several rolls as Neala continued to talk. Recognizing Butter as a man who loved food, she chatted while Butter continued to stare. Tilman couldn't tell if Butter was more smitten with the rolls or with the baker. "I love to bake and so I come in once a week and make fresh rolls." She sat the tray on the counter and placed several large rolls, the icing still warm, in a bag for Butter. Unconsciously, delicately, she licked the icing off her fingers.

"Where might your wife be, Mister . . ."

"Pegram, ma'am, Butter Pegram at your service." He took the rolls, "No wife, ma'am. Never found the right woman"—he paused—"yet."

"Butter," she said with a deep chuckle, "now that's a name a baking woman can appreciate." She placed one hand gently on Butter's arm.

Tilman watched his friend and it took all of his will power not to say something. Butter and the baker talked a few minutes more, and paying for his sweets, Butter tipped his hat and swaggered out the door. At least, Tilman could swear it looked like a swagger.

"Did y' see that gal, Tilman?" Butter mused as he mounted his horse, holding the rolls carefully in one hand. "My, but I'd like t' have time t' get t' know her better." Unwrapping a roll, he reverently bit into it, offering Tilman a bite. "Ooooohhh. This is heaven." Butter continued talking to himself as they headed back to the fort. "Beautiful an' can cook. What's wrong with the fellers around here?"

"Maybe she's been waiting for the right man, Butter," Tilman joked.

"Yes siree, Tilman. Maybe she has."

At mid-morning a four-man crew went about the drill of unhitching the two spans of mules from the ammunition limber and parking it behind the firing line, manhandling the gun carriage up to the firing line while one of the men led the mules fifty yards behind the gun. The mules were so accustomed to the drill that the entire evolution was completed without a single voice command. When all was ready, the Gatling Battery officer, Lieutenant Robert Hunt, introduced himself and invited Tilman and Butter to step up and take a closer look at the gun.

With practiced ease the officer began his lecture. "This is a Model 1866 six-barrel caliber .45-70 Gatling gun." Pointing out each piece as he spoke, he said, "The gun is operated by a hand-driven rotary device, powered by this crank here." He gave the crank a turn that caused the barrels to rotate with a clatter. "The barrels are banded together in a cylinder around a central shaft, and each of the six barrels will be loaded and fired in a single revolution." Since neither Tilman nor Butter asked a question, he warmed to his subject. "Loading of the cartridges is done by simple gravity feed from one of these tin magazines mounted on top of the gun. The gun can fire up to three hundred and fifty rounds every minute."

"Well now, how 'bout you tell me in plain English exac'ly what is it that it does when you turn that handle?" Butter asked.

"Look here, sir," Hunt said. "Turning the crank rotates the central shaft all the barrels are fixed on. Starting the revolution at the top, a cartridge falls into the carrier; the cam pushes the lock and the cartridge into the chamber and holds it while it's fired. Then the next barrel comes up and the cycle is repeated. When a barrel with a fired cartridge gets to the bottom, the cam pulls back the lock and gravity causes the spent case to fall out on the ground. Is that clear?"

"I ain't here to buy it. Maybe you'd best get on with it and show me."

The officer nodded and the man designated as the

gunner, Corporal Brown, and his loader stepped up to the gun. Brown was a balding man in his early fifties and had been watching Butter closely with an amused smile on his lips. His loader placed a magazine filled with twenty cartridges into the feed port and the Brown turned the crank slowly, traversing the gun as he fired. With slow but steady and ear-ringing reports, the gun belched clouds of gray smoke and two hundred yards away several paper targets were shredded by the heavy slugs, and clods of muddy dirt were thrown into the air.

When the noise and echoes died away, Butter whistled in disbelief.

"You were Johnny Rebs, weren't you?" Brown growled at Tilman and Butter.

"We was," Butter simply stated.

"Thought so. Were you at Gettysburg?"

"Both of us were," Tilman said.

"I was too," Brown answered, "Cemetery ridge, on the third day."

"Glad you Yankees didn't bring one these to the ball that day," Butter said, "or they'd been a sight more of us went under the sod up yonder."

"I reckon the war's over. How about I buy you a drink over at the sutler's store after retreat today?" Brown suggested. "We can talk about the old days."

"I'll be there," Butter answered with a laugh. "Maybe in the telling we will win this time!"

Chapter Seventeen

"The men are leaving in the morning. Gordon was going over supplies with Sergeant Leoni." Sally looked worried as the small group of quilters gathered around the Lone Star quilt, each one there well aware of the critical importance of passing time. "I feel like we should be doing something. Every time I think about those two girls . . ."

"Hope they aren't too late." Nettie yanked a thread on the quilt frame, tilting the frame. The ladies on the other side grabbed hold in order that the quilt should not fall on the floor. "Hear they sell those girls down in Mexico City all the time. They love women with that white-blond hair like Maddie's."

"Nettie! What a thing to say." Susannah tried to understand that Nettie had a hard time, what with being bitter with her husband for his drinking, but sometimes she had to work hard at forgiveness. "I think Mr. Wagner has been friends with Captain Law for a long time. Gordon said they grew up together in North Carolina."

"I heard Mr. Valenzuela, the man from the bandits, said they have until Christmas. That is nearly a month." Susannah tried to sound positive.

"You believe the word of a bandit, that's fine with me." Nettie stood up and went to get a cup of coffee. "Personally, I think Miss Maddie got what she deserved."

"Nettie! That's uncalled for. All Maddie did was try to escort Lomida to get some help and this is what's come of it. Not a soul is to blame and you know that." Susannah paused. "Will you pass me the thread please?"

Turning to Sally, Susannah pressed on. "These sweet rolls are wonderful. You have to let me know how you got them so sweet. They have a taste that I don't recognize."

"I used some prickly pear centers, well cooked, and it makes a sweet sauce. Indian Annie showed me how to do that last week. It's wonderful isn't it?" The conversation returned to food, children, letters from far away, and Nettie was left alone with her anger for a companion.

The sound of thread pulling through cloth, rustling petticoats, and Sally's humming was punctuated by the measured sound of gunfire echoing across the post from the canyon.

Law's cook and housekeeper was an Apache girl from the San Carlos Reservation. Because no one could pronounce her name she became simply Indian Annie.

Dark-complexioned, Annie stood barely five-feet tall, with a stocky, bow-legged build. Annie thought her age to be around sixteen years. Her long black hair was tied back by a colorful strip of cloth. A quick learner around the kitchen, Annie soon surprised everybody as she quickly became a wonderfully creative cook. Lomida coached her in English, and the two developed a close if unlikely bond of friendship, with almost constant female chatter and laughter filling the house. Indian Annie came from very little but she was always happy and full of hope and good humor. With the exception of Nettie Wordsmith, who trusted no one, especially an Indian, the post ladies had adopted her and were frequently dropping by to offer advice and check on her.

The dining room in Law's quarters was small, and made even smaller when Law, Tilman, Butter, and Sol Burney crowded around the table. Butter had arrived after everyone else and brought the smell of whiskey. "Talked to that gunner 'til I was blue in the face. We still lost," he muttered.

The men went over last-minute details before their planned departure at first light. Annie prepared venison stew and the men were soon sopping the last traces of the delicious gravy from their bowls with strips of fried bread. Preoccupied as they were, Tilman and Butter still couldn't help but notice that Annie was more than normally attentive to Sol Burney, smiling, offering more stew, refilling his water glass, watching his every move. If any of the others present had even considered the possibility, they would have seen that the girl was taken with the handsome young lieutenant. The men took their coffee in the parlor, where Sol excused himself early.

"Goodnight, gentlemen. I have to see to my men."

When he left, a disappointed Annie busied herself inside cleaning up after the supper and then working in the kitchen, separate from the main house.

"John, I think your Indian girl's sweet on Mr. Burney," Tilman said.

"Nonsense!"

"He's right." Butter laughed. "She looked at him th' way a gal named Slats mooned over Tilman up in Colorado!"

"Poor child. I doubt Burney knows she's alive. Right now, doing his job is all he sees or thinks about." John stood. "Annie is usually full of joy, but she misses Lomida. They were very close."

John's orderly came from the back of the house; he had picked up mail from the eastbound stage. On top of a stack of official correspondence was a letter for Tilman. Butter took the letter, smelling the envelope. "Lavender. 'Minds me of what Catherine wears."

Tilman sat his coffee cup on a side table, a smile on his face. "You going to stand there and smell it or let me have it to read?"

Butter pretended to examine the address. "Well, le' me see." He laughed out loud at the expression on Tilman's face. "Boy, you're worse than I thought. Here." Butter handed him the letter. Butter was right. It did smell like Catherine, fresh and like fields of lavender.

"Guess I'll call it a day, gentlemen." Tilman didn't even notice the amused expressions of the other two men as he quickly disappeared into the evening and the mournful notes of "Taps" echoed across the post, a signal for lights out, the end of another day. The post dogs set up a howling, as usual.

* * *

Alone in his room, Tilman opened the letter, memories sliding out from the opened envelope.

Dear Tilman,

I hope that this letter finds you and doesn't end up at the wrong place. I addressed it to you through your friend John. James pesters me every day about when you are coming back. He said to tell you he takes good care of Needles. James rides him when he returns from school and if he keeps grooming him, I declare Needles' coat is going to fall out.

Pastor Fry came through last night on his way to preach in Granite. He said you should be soon getting to Fort Davis and then you will take care of everything. John is very lucky to have a friend who will help him with his dreadful trouble. I pray every night for the safety of those two young women.

How is Butter? We were all surprised he decided to leave and go with you, but I think he finds a kindred spirit and I know he loves an adventure, and Tilman Wagner you do seem to draw adventure.

I am making some of the yeast bread that you like so. When you return I will fix a batch for you. These are for James to take to a school elocution contest. He is doing a short poem he learned. Before you came and helped him he would have been too shy.

Take care,

Catherine

PS How are your ribs?

* * *

Sleep would not come. Tilman lay awake in the silent darkness, staring at the ceiling. Thoughts of Catherine faded. His optimism regarding the possibility of successfully rescuing Lomida and the schoolteacher deserted him. To find them in such a vast and hostile land was one thing, but getting the two of them safely away from those people was, to be frank, all but impossible. Vicious, cold-blooded killers were holding an innocent girl and her teacher in another country, men with not one iota of a conscience nor human decency. If they hadn't already sold them, or worse, they might decide to kill the two young women before he could get to them.

A question crept into his mind, again, the same question that had been there for days. Could he do it? What if he got Butter killed in this thing, or that young officer, Burney, and his men? Doubt came to Tilman in the night and with it the fear of failing, a consequence he would have to live with for the rest of his life. Suddenly he remembered he was no longer alone, and he crawled out of bed and got down on his knees on the hard, rough plank floor and asked for help from a higher source. They had to rescue the girls and that was that. They could do it. He crawled back into bed. A sense of peace calmed him and he slept.

Chapter Eighteen

In the middle of the night, Maddie woke to the sound of Lomida groaning in pain. Tossing and turning in her sleep, Lomida seemed in the throes of a nightmare.

"Miss Maddie. I don't feel so well."

"Let me feel your head. Do you have a fever? Oh, Lomida, you're burning up. When did you start to feel sick?"

"I don't know. Soon after supper maybe . . ."

Maddie reached under the edge of her skirt for a torn place on her petticoat and ripped off a small piece. She folded and wet it with cool water from the *olla* and she placed the compress on Lomida's brow. She had nothing else in the room to use, nothing else to do. The place they were held prisoner in, little more than a cage of river reeds tied together with gravel on the ground, measured barely five feet by five feet, with not even space to stretch out. Maddie could not stand erect under the low ceiling. A pot in one corner served for necessities.

A torn piece of *serape* lay on top of the straw mattress and a dirty saddle blanket provided cover. It smelled so strongly that Maddie and Lomida used it only in the predawn cold before the sun rose in the sky. It was a far cry from the room she used behind the schoolhouse.

There were no windows or even a real door in their prison. Wind whistled through the loosely lashed reeds. Maddie scooted over to the opening of the lean-to, pulled the cloth that served as a door to one side and looked out. In the firelight she saw one of Chuy's men, looking pale and weak, crossing the courtyard in short but quick steps.

"Aiee, mi estomago."

Maddie understood that. The sound of retching behind the opposite shack wasn't hard to interpret. Maddie thought quickly: *Lomida is sick, and those men are sick, too, but I'm fine.* They must have eaten something that she had not. The meat! Some thing or creature that had a smell Maddie didn't care for. She had refused supper even though it meant going to bed hungry. Now she realized that she had done the right thing.

"Lomida. Did you have some of that meat? I thought I told you not to eat any."

"I know Miss Maddie. Don't be angry at me." Tears flooded Lomida's eyes and ran down flushed cheeks. "I was so hungry. I knew it smelled bad but I didn't care." She cried quietly as Maddie tried to settle her down.

"Hush, Lomida. Hush. I'm not angry."

Just then, Lomida's face closed in humiliation. "I have to . . ."

Dysentery.

Maddie knew that tainted food often caused dysentery. She needed something to stop the illness before it dehydrated Lomida. Already weakened, Lomida lacked the strength to simply endure while the dysentery ran its course. The girl could die.

"Help." Maddie stuck her head out of the opening of the shed. "*Help!*"

"What is it?" Luis appeared out of the cave carrying a lantern. He appeared to be grumpier than usual. Maddie knew he had disappeared for several days but he had ridden back into camp yesterday and seemed in a good mood. "What is wrong with you? Are you sick too?" His tone of voice suggested weary frustration.

Impatiently Maddie shook her head. "I'm fine. Lomida is not, and we must empty the night bucket." She had to get something to help Lomida. "How many of your people are ill?"

Luis looked at her. "Enough. Why?"

"I think I can help all of the sick if you let me get out to a cottonwood tree. Indian Annie over at the fort taught me some cures used by her family and she swears by cottonwood bark tea to take care of dysentery."

Luis started to object but another of his men went by him seeking the outskirts of the camp moaning with each hurried step. "Okay. I go with you. But one false move, *mi senorita querida* . . ." Belying his words of endearment, Luis made a slashing motion across his neck with his hand.

"Don't threaten me, Mr. Valenzuela. You need Lomida healthy and you need me in order to get your money don't you?" Maddie feigned nonchalance although she trembled inside. She had to help Lomida even if it meant helping their captors as well. Another thought overwhelmed her. What if she didn't know what she was doing? What if she ended up making everybody worse or possibly killing them? She had to succeed. There was no other answer. Annie had taught her well. She could do this.

While Luis waited, Maddie cleaned the night bucket and replaced it in the hut for Lomida; she crawled out of the lean-to after telling Lomida to rest until she returned. She stood and stretched. Every muscle in her body hurt. She wasn't used to the forced inactivity that accompanied their confinement in the small hut that was their prison.

"Luis, you want me take woman?" Comes From War came out of the darkness to stand near, the barely controlled lust apparent on his dark, brooding face as he took in Maddie's disheveled appearance. "She Icimanipi-Wihapawin."

"What does that mean?" Luis asked, impatient with the surly warrior.

"It mean 'travels beautiful woman.'" Comes From War reached out to touch, caress, Maddie's shoulder as he circled, appraising her the way a man does a horse. "Maybe I buy from Chuy." Recoiling in disgust, Maddie stepped closer to Luis. She knew she couldn't afford to be alone with Comes From War. Luis apparently read Comes From War as well.

"No. She is too valuable."

Comes From War muttered under his breath and stomped off in the other direction.

"I think he is wanting you, *querida*." Luis laughed aloud as he and Maddie stepped out of the compound and walked down the rocky path. In the weak light cast by the lantern Maddie stumbled several times. Luis muttered about being surrounded with idiots, sick people and a hot-blooded Indian crazy for one woman. At last they came to a line of cottonwood trees by the small stream where the camp got its water.

"There. That's what I need." Maddie had Luis take his knife and shave off the rough gray outer bark of an old cottonwood tree and then she showed him the thin brownish grey inner bark she needed. "Quickly, let's get back to the fire. I'll need a big pot and some water as well."

Luis bristled, and stood there looking at her like she had grown wings. Apparently Luis Valenzuela wasn't used to a woman giving him orders.

"Sorry, Mr. Valenzuela. I forgot myself."

He nodded, relaxing.

"If you will have someone get water and a pot I can make this tea."

Back at the camp Luis motioned to one of the camp women who was adding sticks to the fire, telling her to get a pot and water. Maddie crushed the cottonwood bark and dropped it in the water, stirring it with a stick. The mixture was soon swirling slowly in the pot, small bubbles appeared, and it took on an unappealing yellow tinge, then came to a full rolling boil. The fumes made a person's eyes sting.

"This smells horrible. It's bound to work," Luis looked over Maddie's shoulder and joked, then remembered who he was talking to and became stern once again.

Maddie soon moved the bitter tea from the fire to cool and fixed a cup to take to Lomida. She touched it to her lips to test it, judged it to be cool enough. She hoped it would work. Luis sent one of the camp women to have the sick men drink the remaining tea.

Morning found Lomida's dysentery stopped and the

men from the camp no longer moaning. Maddie decided that everybody would survive and promptly fell into a well-deserved sleep.

"Miss Maddie. Get up." Lomida tugged on her arm.

"What . . . ?" Maddie pulled herself from sleep into the reality of midmorning and smells of unwashed humanity, away from a beautiful dream . . . she wore a blue gown, shiny . . .

"Come on. Mr. Valenzuela says come on and you know he isn't very patient."

Hearing the fear in Lomida's voice, Maddie rubbed the sleep from her eyes, the blue dress floating away into oblivion even as she looked around the crude room they shared.

"What . . ."

"We haven't got all day. There is much to do. *Arriba,* hurry . . ." Luis Valenzuela's head poked through the cloth door cover. "Don't be modest, *querida.* Get your things and come with me. I am a busy man."

Lomida and Maddie hastily grabbed their few belongings and crawled out. Luis stood there smoothing his mustache as usual. Maddie reassured herself that Lomida, though wobbly, was fine. The cottonwood bark had definitely done the trick.

"What is the problem, Mr. Valenzuela? We haven't done . . ."

Luis stopped at one of the more substantial lean-tos that were built into the side of the canyon wall. An older Mexican woman Maddie had not seen before stepped out of the hut and motioned for the girls to enter. "*Buenos días*" she said. She touched Maddie's arm. "You doctor?" She pointed to herself proudly. "*Soy doctor también.*"

Maddie looked to Luis. "What?"

"She says she is a doctor too. Diosune Benavides is called a *curandera* and she has lived in these hills for many years. Chuy sent for her last night, but she was not here. She was delivering a new baby up on top of the mesa. She knows many of the healing trees and plants." Luis showed them into the larger room. "Lucky for you, Miss Maddie, that she was gone."

"I don't understand . . ." Maddie looked confused and Luis relented.

"Last night not only did the little *gringa* and several of my men eat the bad meat, but also Chuy, and when Chuy gets sick he is one mean *hombre*." Luis paused. "When you told me about the tea I gave him some to drink and he felt better in a very short time. He was pleased with me and so, I am pleased with you."

"But I still don't understand."

"This is to be your new home. Here with Diosune. It is larger, better built and you can even stand as you notice. Diosune will keep an eye on you for us. But . . ."—Luis started out the door—"if you try to escape I will hunt you down and stake you to a pole."

Chapter Nineteen

Maddie and Lomida looked at what was to be their new home. The room was twice the size of the lean-to and Diosune had put a picture of the Virgin Mary in a small niche in the wall. There was a smoke hole in the roof and a fire pit in the middle of the room to keep the damp out, and Maddie's bones welcomed that little treat. Diosune motioned for Lomida to join her by the fire. She reached behind the child, bringing forth a small woven basket that smelled like heaven.

"*Mija?*" With a mother's term of endearment for her daughter she offered a fresh hot corn tortilla to Lomida who quickly took one, almost dropping it.

"*Cuidado. Es caliente,* eh . . . hot!" Diosune offered one to Maddie, who wasted no time in consuming hers. It was hard to tell Diosune's age. Years of living in primitive conditions had turned her skin a dark, weathered brown. Wrinkles crisscrossed her face while lively brown eyes missed nothing. Diosune sat straight, a proud healer respected by her people; she appeared at peace with her surroundings.

"*Gracias,* Diosune." Maddie sat down, noticing that here, the blankets were old but had been dusted, and though faded they were much better than the filth they had just left. Examining her new prison, Maddie saw dried plants hanging from the ceiling, several of which she recognized. They added a pleasant fragrance to the room. She saw sage and basil but there were others plants she did not know. Maddie pointed to a long spiky cactus. She made a questioning motion to Diosune, who sat on her small stool by the fire.

"*Ocotillo.*" Diosune pretended to draw a knife and cut her arm, pantomimed mixing the cactus and water and placing it on the cut. Lomida watched the charade and giggled. Diosune looked at her and then grinned, showing a lovely smile that was minus a front tooth. Apparently there wasn't a dentist in Ayala's bed of thieves.

The days passed with Maddie, Lomida and Diosune playing a game of charades as they learned about the plants that hung around the room, each picking up words in the other's language. Yucca for sore joints— arthritis. Dandelion to help with difficult breathing and congestion; sagebrush for tea, snakebites and boils, for a short time the two girls forgot where they were as Diosune demonstrated some of the cures that had been used for hundreds of years by the people of the Chihuahuan desert. The best one was when Diosune took some of the yucca and showed them how to wash their hair. After wetting Lomida's hair, Diosune broke open the heart of a yucca plant and rubbed it into Lomida's red hair and then rinsed it with a bucket of spring water. The yucca left Lomida's hair smelling clean and soft. Lomida and Diosune then made a show of washing Maddie's blond hair, much to Maddie's delight. They had settled down around the fire when a knock on the woven beargrass door prompted Maddie to get up from the fire pit. The reed frame that held the door was primitive but far better than the torn blanket that had protected them before.

Maddie opened the door and found a basket. Pulling it into the room, she looked inside. Clothing! Dresses for them both. There were even several cotton petticoats and a couple of pairs of bloomers as well. One of the dresses was serviceable Wedgwood blue with a corset of darker blue.

"The lady I worked for in Missouri called corsets 'stays' because of all the whalebone that is sewn into them," Maddie said. "She said it was good for women to have extra support, but I think they're really uncomfortable."

"I'm glad I don't have to wear a corset," Lomida said.

Then Maddie pulled a gaudy red dress out of the pack. It was soft and made of velvet. It was apparently a ball gown, as it had a very revealing front. She held it up to herself and sighed, picturing a different time and place.

"Miss Maddie. You can't wear that out or you might be arrested!" Lomida giggled. "It's like those the officers' ladies wear to the dances at Fort Davis only theirs have more on top. Missus Wordsmith would even be short on words." Lomida tried to look sternly at Maddie. "It will never do for everyday things, like doing the wash." They both laughed at the picture of a disapproving Nettie Wordsmith.

"I agree, Lomida. It would not meet her idea of acceptability at all." It was a bit much. However, Maddie needed an extra dress. She looked puzzled until Diosune motioned to them. From a basket she kept by her chair, came a dark wine shawl. Although the shawl appeared several shades darker than the dress, it would definitely offer cover to Maddie. She handed it to Maddie, apparently glad to help.

"*Gracias*, again, Diosune. What would we do without you?"

"What do you have for me, Miss Maddie?" Lomida took a green-checked dress with a dark green apron and a yellow day dress, full sleeves and a fairly full skirt. Bouncing unsteadily around, she examined the clothing. "Where do you think these dresses came from?"

"I think it best we count our blessings and not worry too much about the history of these clothes." Maddie held Lomida's new clothing up to her small frame. The dress swallowed the child. Rummaging through the basket she found a real treasure. "Look here." The small box she held revealed needles and thread. "You can wear the green dress while I take up the yellow one."

The dirt and dust on the clothing they had been wearing for the last few weeks had left them grimy and they both knew they smelled. After a moment, Maddie came to a decision. "We are truly a mess, young lady. Maybe we can get Diosune to help us once more."

Turning to Diosune, Maddie pantomimed bathing. Diosune quickly nodded understanding and disappeared out the door. The two girls heard Diosune speaking rapid Spanish to two of the other camp women and a short time later, a dented but still useable two-gallon metal bucket of warm water appeared at the front of the lean-to and the two girls gladly dragged it inside and sponged off the worst of the dirt and sweat. When they had finished cleaning up, Diosune gave Maddie and Lomida some aloe leaves, broke them so that the clear sap oozed out. Next, she showed them how to apply the aloe on their faces and necks to soften the skin and to keep the sun from burning them.

The green dress was short enough for Lomida to wear but its former owner had carried several more pounds than little Lomida, so Maddie had to baste an extra seam in the side so Lomida wouldn't get lost in the extra material. A fairly stylish bustle was removed and used to make a sash to help keep the garment on Lomida's slight frame.

"I don't think I'll win a beauty contest"—Lomida twirled around—"but it's nice to be clean again."

Wearing the red gown and shawl, Maddie thanked Diosune once again, promptly dumping their old clothing into the bath water to wash. Diosune pulled from her cache of herbs the root of an agave plant that had been shredded to make a soap substitute. It was wonderful.

As the evening wore on Lomida fell asleep from sheer exhaustion while Diosune kept busy weaving a basket in the corner of the room. A knock at the door, a rapid exchange in Spanish, and Diosune took her healer's basket and disappeared.

For the first time in many days, Maddie realized that she did not feel like a prisoner. She knew a guard was outside when Diosune left the building, but she didn't feel so threatened. She'd had to fend for herself for most of her life. Was there ever a time when she had not? Not since her parents had died.

"Miss Maddie? Are you awake?"

"I thought you were asleep, Lomida." Maddie looked at the small girl. Dark rings encircled her blue eyes. "You need to sleep."

"What were you thinking about?"

"My parents. I was thinking that I was your age when my folks died of typhoid fever. We were in Independence, Missouri, getting ready to go west like everybody else."

"Did you have relatives to go live with? Or brothers and sisters?"

"No, Lomida. There was just me. They put me in an orphanage."

"Ooh. That's horrible. Did you like . . . ?"

"I hated it. I ran away at eighteen when I realized I was going to be free help if I didn't."

No reason to tell Lomida about the way the boys watched a young, pretty girl.

"Well. What did you do then?"

"I went to work with a family on a wagon train headed for Dodge City, Kansas. They had three small children and so I stayed with them for a few years, and finally got a job at a dry goods store." Maddie smiled. "I was good with numbers and could read and write and that helped a lot. That's where I met Lieutenant Samuel Minear."

Samuel Minear had been a young Second Lieutenant at Fort Larned. He had courted Maddie for a little over a year before he got reassigned to Fort Davis since the Army was closing Fort Larned.

Lomida leaned against Maddie's shoulder. "That's why you came to Fort Davis wasn't it?"

"Yes, Lomida, that's how I ended up in the corner of

Texas out in the wilderness." Maddie was to meet Samuel and marry him at Fort Davis. Arriving by stage, she found instead that Samuel had been killed while on patrol the week before her arrival. It seemed to Maddie that God had stood her up once again.

Not knowing what to do or where to go, Maddie found herself unexpectedly in the job of schoolmarm since the Fort Davis schoolmistress had eloped in the middle of the year. Maddie knew then that she was alone and it was up to her to make the most of her life.

"Any more questions, Miss Busybody?"

Silence met her question and Maddie found that Lomida was fast asleep. She stirred, rubbing her bad leg even in her dreams. Maddie lay awake, staring at the ceiling lit only by a few glowing coals left in the fire pit. She had to get them out of this mess. She had to figure out where they were and how to get safely back home.

Chapter Twenty

The ammunition limber and gun carriage slowed the march as the small party made its way southwest across rocky, rough ground following a trail flanked by knobby hills; a broken wheel would mean an unwelcome delay. To the west, Blue Mountain was visible on the horizon. At times the route was easy, but some parts of the trail passed dangerously through low-growing clumps of "horse crippler" cactus that gave Tilman and Butter cause to wonder what Smith was thinking. Twice the limber and gun had to be roped and carefully let down steep bluffs capped by ancient lava flows along stream courses and then hauled slowly up the opposite sides, a time-consuming effort.

"We ain't makin' time. Wonderin' if that feller knows his trails as good as Law said," Butter muttered to Tilman, then spat a brown stream of tobacco juice and wiped his chin with the back of his gloved hand.

"For a scout Smith stays almighty close to us," Tilman observed. "Butter, drop back and ride drag.

Watch our back trail and keep a sharp eye. I'm goin' to ride point." Tilman spurred his cavalry mount, a hard-muscled and spirited roan, alongside Smith. The big man had opened his canteen, tilted his head back and was pouring water into his eyes, rubbing them, as if he was trying to clear dust from them. "We're headin' just west of south, so I think I'll take a look out ahead of us," and before Smith could answer, Tilman rode away.

About a mile in front of the small Army detachment Tilman began to cut for sign, swinging his horse on a wide arc across what ground he figured their line of march would follow. At a low ridge to the west he found what he had expected—fresh boot prints among some boulders offering a good view of the plains. Someone had very recently sat among those rocks long enough to smoke several cigarettes. A man had been sent there to watch, most likely to see if the gun was coming down the trail as Luis had demanded. When the watcher saw them coming with the gun, he walked down the other side to where he'd left his horse. Whoever it was rode away to the southwest, in the direction of Lajitas.

Tilman rode down to wait for the patrol to reach him. He called Butter forward and took Burney, Leoni and Smith aside. "They know we're coming, and they'll probably be watching from here on in," Tilman said, explaining what he'd seen in the rocks.

Smith turned and squinted into the afternoon sun, but said nothing.

"D'you think they'll try to take the gun before we get to Lajitas?" Burney asked.

"I expect so," Tilman said. "If they can take us out here, they can have the gun and still sell the girls. Let's surprise them."

"I know what you're a-thinkin'. They'll be expectin' us to ride into Lajitas like good little soldier boys," Butter observed. "So let's us not do that."

"What do you mean?" Burney asked.

"Why, let's not be foolish enough to *give* 'em th' gun like a Christmas present," Butter said. "Let's change th' game."

"Smith, here's what we need. D'you know of a good place for us to hole up a few miles from Lajitas, a good defensive position where we can see the trails and they can't get at us without exposing themselves?"

"I know a place like that," Leoni said, "at the foot of the Mesa de Anguila."

"Eel Mesa? Out here in the desert?" Tilman asked.

"Yeah, I reckon it's called that because the local folks catch eels out of the Rio Bravo along there."

"Well, let's go take a look. If it's good we can fort up and Butter and I'll go find Valenzuela, and arrange the trade. Maybe I can figure a way to turn the tables and take the girls away from them."

They stopped while it was still daylight at a place called Alamito Creek where Leoni knew they could find sweet water. The further south they went, the harder good water would be to find. It tended to be gyppy in most places, and bad water would tear up a man's belly. The men were in a good mood, glad to be away from the endless stable and work details under the watchful gaze of petty tyrants at the fort. Their horses were also eager for the trail, sound of wind and limb and easy to care for. The men thought it good to be doing something that promised danger and the excitement of action. Sitting on the porch was for granma and granpappy; they enlisted to fight.

The men rested, refilled canteens and the water kegs strapped to the ammunition limber, and boiled coffee and cooked Army bacon as they squatted around small fires. Leoni had soaked dry beans in water all day in an iron Dutch oven on the limber. The oven now sat in the hot coals and the simmering beans would make a good breakfast the following morning. Leoni passed around crackers from a box of Army bread strapped to the limber chest—hard tack—that was dated 1865. The Army never threw away anything that might be of possible use! Mr. Burney used a pocketknife to try to pick the weevils out of his crackers.

"Leave 'em there," Butter advised with a laugh, "they don't eat much and man shouldn't never turn down fresh meat when he can get it!"

"A man could break a tooth on these," Burney complained in disgust, "so how do those worms manage?"

"See how the soldiers break up the crackers to soften them in their coffee?" Tilman asked. "That's the best way to eat your tack, even better at night when you can't see the bugs floating in the cup."

"Rider comin' in," one of the soldiers said.

The men stood, weapons at hand, and looking in the direction the soldier pointed. No one noticed as Tilman drew his pistol and then eased himself into a shallow dry wash for cover, a little extra security until the unknown rider's intentions became clear.

"Hello the camp!"

"Show your hands and come on in," Burney answered.

The rider picked his way through the brush and stopped at the edge of the camp. He sat a fine-looking, deep-chested stallion, dark-skinned with a coat the color of steel dust, and a pack mule on a short lead. The man showed empty hands.

"Get down. Coffee's hot and you're welcome to some grub," Butter called.

"Thank you," the man said as he dismounted and walked to the fire where he squatted on his haunches, shifted his belted Colt to a more comfortable location, and accepted the tin cup of steaming hot coffee Butter offered. The man drank it down and poured himself another. There was an animal alertness about the way the stranger's eyes surveyed the camp, yet he seemed to be at ease with his surroundings at the same time. The men watched the newcomer curiously. What kind of a man could take boiling coffee from a pot and finish it with relish and be ready for another? The young soldiers were used to rough men on the frontier, but this was a man of a different sort.

"Howdy, Wagner," the stranger said, rising.

"Gillette," Tilman said, holstering his pistol and coming over to shake hands. "Last I heard you were over at San Saba. You were with Tays' company, I believe."

"And you was a-ridin' a hard trail. Baylor told me your boy was killed, an' said you'd gone to Colorado to find the feller done it."

"I found him."

"Figgered you would." After a moment's contemplation Gillette said, "I'm a mite tired of corn dodgers. A lightnin' storm a couple o' nights back spooked my mule an' the fool animal run off and I like to never caught him. The dad-lem pack come loose an' scattered most o' m' grub across the prairie. By the time I found it come mornin' the coyotes done et most of it."

"We can spare you some," Burney said. "Sergeant Leoni, get a slab of bacon and some coffee and beans for Mr. Gillette."

"I'm much obliged."

"Lieutenant Burney," Tilman said by way of introduction, "this is Sergeant J. B. Gillette and he's a Texas Ranger."

"What brings you out this way?"

"Me an' eight other boys come with Lieutenant Baylor to set up a ranger camp at Ysleta, for there's been some unpleasantness with Apaches over that way," the ranger answered. "I taken a prisoner to Fort Stockton an' I'm a-headin' back to camp." Indicating the Gatling, he continued, "An' you, what're you draggin' that hardware around here for?"

Tilman explained as Butter sliced bacon into a skillet over the fire and Gillette sat quietly. Tilman finished his story as Gillette chewed his bacon and hard tack. "I heard about the raid on the station, an' them runnin' off with the passengers. I heard too they was in Old Mexico. You reckon you can do any good?"

"If they're still alive, we'll find them, and if we find them, we'll get them back."

Gillette was quiet. "Reckon I'd best drift."

Gillette rode west and later, after full dark, the rescue party packed up and moved about two miles away from the fires of their supper camp, and picked a site among thick scrub brush to sleep after setting the guard detail. In the darkness Butter came and sat by Tilman.

"While I was a-helpin' Gillette load that mule, he tol' me a thing or two about this feller Smith that's a-guidin' us, an' you ain't gonna like it."

"Go on."

"Gillette says th' Army over at Fort McKavett paid him off. They said Smith's eyes is fadin'."

"He's going blind?"

"He never said that. But, his eyes is weak, an' he ain't reliable. Said he misses too much sign, and it'll get somebody killed one o' these days."

Tilman was quiet. "Butter, I've heard of people losing their sight after a head wound. You don't suppose when I knocked Smith in the head I could have done it?"

"No tellin'. Listen, you can't know if you did or you didn't cause his eyes to fail. What I understand is you never had no choice at the time. If you hadn't chunked him in th' head he'd have killed your prisoner, an' he could have killed you too."

"Thanks, Butter."

"I've heard of the snow blindin' folks up in Colorado, an' I once seen a feller blind from it, so I don't reckon it's any different out here on some of these salt flats, the goin' blind from the glare I mean."

"It's possible," Tilman said. "Anyway, you and I have to be especially alert, but let's us keep this to ourselves for now."

Since leaving Alamito Creek the land had changed to a series of stream-cut terraces across a gravel plain. Even the sparse scrubby junipers became smaller and sparser. Near noon of the third day out from the fort, Tilman rode beside Burney at the head of the small

Army patrol. The land sloped gradually down toward the Rio Grande River to their front.

"Over to east of us that line of reeds and brush is Terlingua Creek," Leoni pointed out, "and maybe two miles to the west, you'll find good water at Comanche Spring. This trail we're following is the western track of the Comanche War Trail to Mexico."

Smith now rode about a quarter of a mile in front of the main body of the patrol, on point, heading for a box canyon at the foot of a high ridge Leoni pointed out as Eel Mesa. Titanic forces at work within the earth over hundreds of thousands of years had caused the long but narrow mesa to be lifted high above the desert floor while the forces of wind and water combined to tear it down, creating rocky talus slopes which fanned out below the steep front wall of the mountain. Here and there canyons cut the front, some extending several hundred feet into the wall.

Smith followed a dry stream bed that led into one of the canyons, and Tilman watched as he disappeared from view around a bend. Tilman and Butter were awed by the harsh ruggedness of the land around them as they constantly watched for the rider who they were sure shadowed them from a distance, reporting their every move.

"The Indians here say that after he had finished making the stars, the world and things that live on the earth, the Great Spirit took all the leftovers he couldn't use anywhere else and piled them here, where the river makes it's big bend," Leoni explained. "That's Mexico over there behind the mesa, maybe a mile or so." The conversation was shattered by the sudden ragged pop of distant gunfire.

"Look yonder!"

Smith reappeared around the bend of the dry wash, whipping his horse with his reins and spurring hard. Three Indians, their terrifying war cries shrill in the quiet afternoon air, followed him.

"There, that little knoll! Sergeant, take cover there!" Burney shouted as he pointed to a low hill a few hundred yards away. Needing no further orders the driver of the gun limber and carriage wheeled his mules and whipped them forward, following the lieutenant. Leoni, Tilman and Butter drew rifles from saddle sheaths and followed behind.

"Where's he a-goin'? Can't he see us?" Butter asked with consternation. Then his voice boomed across the desert, "Smith, over here!" and Smith turned and rode toward the knoll, the Indians gaining on the lone rider.

"Let's cover him," Tilman said, levering a cartridge into his Winchester and firing at the Indian closest to Smith. He missed. Butter fired, and missed as well, but the Indians slowed, surprised by the sudden appearance of other white men. The Apaches held up to study the situation.

"Hey, look!" one of the troopers shouted. "There's more!"

From the canyon came more Indians, riding hard.

"I count twenty-one," said Leoni, coolly.

"Unlimber!" Burney commanded. "Get that gun up and ready. Sergeant, place the gunners on the reverse slope to cover the rear approaches. Tie off those mules!" Burney's pale blue eyes glowed with the excitement of his first Indian action. "Tilman, Butter, if you'll take the flanks and cover the gunners, we'll open the ball!"

"Hot dang, if he ain't one to ride the river with!"

Butter shouted as he piled rocks to make a small fort. "'Minds me o' you, Tilman!"

"Ready!" the gunner shouted.

"Hold your fire. Wait for my order." Burney said calmly. Smith pulled his horse to a stop at the knoll, dismounted, and turned to look back at the Indians. He tied his horse to the limber, and reported to Burney.

"They're Apaches!" Smith shouted breathlessly. "Their camp is in that pocket, and they've got maybe fifty head of horses in there. Scared the devil outta me!"

Whips His Horse studied the pitifully small force on the knoll, deciding how best to attack. "Wait," he said. "We will stop here."

"They are few!" a young warrior exclaimed as his pony danced alongside Whips His Horse. "We will kill them all and burn their wagon. We will eat their mules and take many horses and guns from the white men and the black white men."

"I will go there!" Whips His Horse shouted, pointing at the knoll, his excitement and blood lust rising, "Who will follow?"

He kicked his horse into a dead run, saw a swell in the ground that provided some cover for his advance, and swung to the left, perhaps half the Apaches following him. The remainder of the Apaches chose to follow another young warrior. The Apaches thundered into a broad fronted mass, screaming war chants as their run took them in a direct attack toward the knoll.

"They're coming straight in. Man the Gatling, quick now. Steady!" Burney said, his voice shrill with fear as the mass of Indians closed to three hundred yards. "Fire! Fire! Commence firing!"

The hill exploded with the stuttering sound and smoke of the Gatling, Springfield carbines, Winchesters and Burney's pistol which almost drowned out the men's fury of mindless shouts, laughs and curses as the battle opened. The Gatling spewed heavy slugs into the Indian mass, killing and tumbling horses and men to the ground in a shocking display of firepower no Indian had ever seen.

Return fire from the Apaches became scattered and mostly ineffective. However, Burney, in trying to set a good example of fearless leadership, stood during the fight and was staggered by a bullet in the neck. The single buck shot appeared to have come from a shotgun fired several hundred yards away. Luckily for the officer it lacked penetrating power. The ball lodged in the muscle below his left ear, painful but not fatal.

Across the flats, a young warrior was down, killed, along with three other fighters, and six were wounded. Joseph Half Man was one of the wounded, hit in the belly, and would certainly die before the sun set. Ten horses were dead; two others limped off the field wounded. Whips His Horse had suffered a stunning defeat, and roared his anger as he withdrew to the safety of the stream bed. How could so few men shoot so fast? It was a thing he did not understand. He must kill these white men and learn their secret. How did the black white men who stood at the wagon during the fight have the power to shoot that way? Could it be that the wagon had the power to shoot many bullets? He must have that wagon.

From a vantage point on the slopes of nearby Sierra Aguja a man known as Cuchillo Negro, or Black Knife, depending on which side of the border he rode, viewed the battle in the valley. He was Luis Valenzuela's scout, sent to follow the soldiers with the Gatling gun and make sure no other soldiers followed behind to spring a trap on Luis. Black Knife had never seen a Gatling in action, and after the battle understood why such a gun was so important to the revolution. He also saw that the Indians had begun moving nearer the knoll and were encircling it. After dark the Apaches, who preferred to fight on foot, would silently steal close and kill the white men. He must ride, and tell Luis that the Apaches were about to take his gun.

"Lieutenant, I hate to tell you this, but you shouldn't offer such an inviting target," Sergeant Leoni said as Tilman and Butter watched. "There is no glory in making a target of yourself. Nobody doubts your courage. You don't have to prove how brave you are." Leoni kept up the chatter as he used a pair of pliers and a pocketknife to remove the ball from Burney's neck.

"Can you dig it out?" Burney's voice tensed.

"Wait . . . ah, there it is!" Leoni squeezed the lead ball from the hole and handed it to the young officer. Out came the silver flask, and, "This may hurt a little," Leoni poured brandy into the wound.

Burney gritted his teeth and sucked air.

In their hurried departure from the fort no one had thought to bring any medical supplies. The careless error heightened the seriousness of the situation. One that should never have happened. From his saddlebag Leoni pulled the white shirt Artemisia had packed for him—she always boiled his shirts because he liked to have a clean one to change into midway through a patrol—and tore off a strip to bind the wound. "Now, sir, take a drink and don't stand up for a while."

"Well, what are our options?" Burney looked at the small group. "Sergeant?"

"It'll be a fight, sir, but we've got water, food, and ammunition enough for a long fight."

"We've got good cover here," Tilman suggested, "and the approaches are across open ground. They'll pay a price taking us."

A bullet whacked into the dirt near Butter as the Indians began a desultory but galling fire to keep the whites from moving away from cover. Several others followed. The shots, coming from a position about five hundred yards distant, were more accurate than anyone expected.

"One of them Apaches can shoot!" Butter observed. "That ain't a Winchester. More 'n likely they got a Army Springfield. What do you think, Tilman?"

"You can bet on that. Let's pull back to the top of the knoll and fort up. If we kill enough of them maybe they'll figure the cost is too high, and give up."

"Butter?" Leoni asked.

"Tilman's right. We can go to ground and hit 'em, how far out? Them Springfields is good out to six hundred yards, ain't they?"

"That's right. And Tilman, your Winchester's a .45–75; it should be good out about the same distance. Well, let's get set in and see if we can't make things hot for that fellow out there."

Burney was developing a case of the shakes; it had nothing to do with being scared for only a fool was not scared when bullets flew. It came from the stress of his first combat, his first wound. Had he killed one of those Indians? Well, he'd fired, they all had and tumbled some of the Apaches from their horses, but whether he took a life that day was not a certain thing. Still, taking a life played on a man's mind. Some men cried, some shook, some just sat quietly and stared at nothing, and there was no shame in it. Most men needed a little time to think and then get over it. Next time it might be *him*, Sol Burney, that got tumbled in a fight.

Tilman scrambled in a low crawl to a patch of strong smelling chaparral bushes. Taking his knife he hacked off several branches and returned to the hill. Butter watched as Tilman selected a flat stone and a round one, stripped the leaves from the branches and crushed them into small coarse pieces. Moving to sit beside Burney, Tilman removed the cloth covering over his wound and liberally sprinkled the ground bits of the leaves into and around the wound.

"Why are you doing that?"

"I've seen Mexicans use this on cuts. They say it won't go to gangrene if you do this. If it don't cure you at least it won't kill you."

"Do tell," Butter exclaimed, "I never heard of such a thing."

"Sir," Leoni interrupted Burney's thoughts, "we'll have a third quarter moon, coming up around one o'clock, and for sure those Apaches will come after us tonight; with knives."

Burney's neck was becoming more painful with each passing moment. "Okay, two men to a fighting position. One sleeps a couple of hours at dark, the other sleeps until midnight. Nobody sleeps after that." He sounded a lot more confident than he was.

Leoni stood up to go and direct the men to their fighting positions. There followed a hollow smacking sound and with a grunt Leoni fell and lay still. Tilman crawled over to Leoni and saw the entrance wound. A bullet had struck Leoni high on the right side of his back. Tilman turned him over and saw that the bullet had exited just below Leoni's collarbone. Tilman would have to clean the wound as best he could, making sure the bullet took no torn bits of uniform into the hole, for that would surely cause it to fester into gangrene. That is, if the shock of his fishing around in there for debris didn't kill the man. Their situation was worsening by the moment.

Chapter Twenty-one

My dear Tilman,

I am sitting on my front porch this beautiful fall morning wearing a winter coat which is good for the breeze today is quite cold and brisk. Do you remember the two large blue spruce trees that stand in my front yard? This wind causes the needles to turn from dark blue to silver depending on the direction of the sunlight. They are such an unusual color; they almost seem to be hand painted. As usual I am wearing the old pair of leather gloves that I always wear in the morning when doing my chores. You know, the soft ones. They are nearly as old as I am.

I have your latest letter which arrived last night. It is already worn and creased from reading and rereading. Pastor Fry is boarding here for the week as he is preaching a revival in the new town of Buena Vista, or 'beautiful view,' and he is holding church in the harness shop of all places.

Mahonville has officially been renamed, and the townspeople hope it's going to be a more pleasant place to live now that the main troublemakers have been killed, run out of town or exposed and removed from any influence and power. Tilman, you know that is mainly because of you and the people of the town are very grateful.

Pastor Fry just joined me on the porch and wants to know how you are faring. He is having his usual morning coffee. The cold weather seems to agree with him. I explained to Paul that you and Butter are fighting once again for justice. I told him about the bandits that are holding the young girls as hostage. He is worried as time is of the essence but knows that you two and the men from Fort Davis will handle everything. Being an old Cavalry man himself he says to tell you that he is looking forward to hearing more of the buffalo soldiers.

Before Paul went to the stable to feed his horse he asked if I miss you. He told me that James grooms Needles each night and prays that you will return so that I will smile again.

Don't you laugh, Tilman Wagner. I also don't want you to get too sure of yourself. I am closing for now as I see Paul and James returning to the house and know I will not have any peace this morning unless I go fix them some fresh buttermilk pancakes with cane syrup.

Take care and give Butter our best. We all miss you and you know that truth be told I miss you a great deal.

Yours,
Catherine

Chapter Twenty-two

Chuy picked his teeth after a fine supper of roast javalina. Diosune knew how to prepare the meat with chiles so that it was tender and tasty.

Chuy, feeling expansive, ordered, "Old woman, take some of this meat to the white women," as Diosune cleared the plates. He reached down lazily to scratch the ears of his favorite hunting dog.

"Now for a cigar and tequila," Luis said with a loud belch.

"Life is good," Chuy said with a sigh. He looked around, restless as always and spied Julio, one of the few bandits who could play a guitar as well as he could shoot. "Julio! A little music, *por favor*. I feel like a sad song or some *ranchera* music. What do you think, eh?"

Julio smiled—he was always ready to perform—and got his guitar and sat by the fire. Soon the plaintive sounds of the lone guitar echoed across the canyon. In the distance a coyote added his tenor yips to the music and soon one of the women of the camp, Soledad, came over by Julio and started to sing. A large woman, aged beyond her years by hard conditions the *revolucionarios* endured, Soledad began to sing, her low voice weaving magic with the guitar. Chuy closed his eyes and saw once again Soledad as the beautiful, fiery young renegade who had wandered into his camp years before, intent on making things better for her people. Coal-black hair that reached her waist, eyes that flashed as she sang of injustice and righting wrongs. Her spirit and ideas had drawn him to her as a moth to a flame and the two of them became inseparable.

The soft tapping of feet on the dirt caused him to open his eyes and Anna and Celeste, two of the younger women who followed the revolution, were softly dancing on the hard-packed dirt around the fire pit. The men began to clap and the music soon went from slow to fast and faster as the traditional Mexican sounds serenaded the canyon and all of its inhabitants.

"The music is wonderful, isn't it?" Lomida sat at the opening of Diosune's hut. "It makes you want to cry and dance all at the same time."

Maddie wrapped her arms around her knees while she sat quietly beside Lomida, listening to the unexpected entertainment. The red and yellow flames of the fire, the women swirling colorful striped shawls as they danced, constantly weaving intricate patterns around the fire pit were indeed a picture to remember. A stranger wandering in for a night's rest would never know this was a place of renegades and outlaws wanted on both sides of the border.

A sound from behind caused Maddie to turn and peer inside as Diosune quietly motioned to her to look to her right. Turning carefully, Maddie saw Comes

From War in the shadows of the wall staring at her with a burning look that petrified her. Diosune recognized the danger as well for she called Maddie and Lomida to come inside. Although they were back in the hut Maddie thought she could still feel Comes From War's gaze on her. What had she done to beguile the man? Certainly she had done all she could to discourage him. Why did he persist? She was filled with a dreadful and unshakeable sense of foreboding. The music and singing continued long into the night.

"*Mi Jefe,* a rider approaches," a guard shouted from the outlook position above the cave entrance.

The men stood and, followed by the dog, walked to see who it could be as Cuchillo Negro reined his lathered horse to a stop, dismounted and tossed the reins to one of the guards. As he approached Chuy his hand shot out to lift a chunk of meat from the tray by the fireplace. Attacking the meat ravenously, between bites he reported, "There is trouble, *Jefe*. You are in danger of losing the gun. Many Apaches have surrounded the white soldiers near Mesa de Anguilla, and the soldiers are unable to escape."

"Apaches?" Chuy knew that it could not be Lone Wolf. He was raiding across the border in Mexico and was not in Texas. "Where did the Apaches come from? How did they know about my gun?" Chuy took his pistol belt from the back of a chair and buckled it around his waist. "No one is going to get my gun. I need it for the *revolucion*. I have come too far to lose this gun."

Cuchillo Negro grabbed one of the bottles of tequila and washed the cold meat down in one gulp. "They are angry, the Apaches. Whips His Horse leads them. He is the one Luis took the women from. That made them angry, *Jefe*. Now they want that gun. And"—he took another drink of tequila—"they want to be rid of the white soldiers and the black white soldiers as badly as you do." Cuchillo Negro sat down and pulled one of the younger women onto his lap. When he drank, Cuchillo Negro was not a pleasant man.

Chuy motioned the girl to leave and she ran quickly to safety. He sat by the scout trying to understand how things could have gone so badly for him. A short time ago all had been well. Once again the white soldiers were interfering with his plans. He wanted that gun and then he wanted to rid the country of the white men. He didn't care what he had promised; he planned to kill them all. As to the girls, Chuy smiled; they would be sold to the highest bidder. If he kept the little one seated no one would know she had a bad leg and they would buy her for her dark red hair. He would win on all sides. But first he had to go get his gun. The longer he thought the more he stewed. Cuchillo Negro, sensing his mood, took his tequila bottle and slipped into the darkness to follow the girl.

Chuy flew into a sudden rage of frustration and cursing, swung a kick at the dog and missed, almost falling as the dog slunk away. "Get the men, tonight we ride to Lajitas with everyone we have here. Luis! Send someone to bring all my men from the camp at Sierra del Carmen to Lajitas."

Yelling for an irritated Cuchillo Negro, Chuy said, "You will lead us. From Lajitas we will ride before first light and surprise the Apaches at dawn." Cuchillo Negro had unfinished business with the woman but he knew that Chuy was not to be stopped so he tossed the tequila bottle into the flame, and watched the flare as the liquor burned intensely for a brief moment before ebbing.

To no one in particular, Chuy shouted, "My horse!"

Within half an hour a file of eight men, Cuchillo Negro in the lead, followed by Chuy and Luis, was threading its way in the fading light of evening along the narrow trail down through the canyon, bound for Lajitas.

Tilman was awakened by the pebbles Butter tossed at him. On the trail or in a dangerous situation no man touched another to awaken him, for a human touch could cause a sleeping man to awaken with a start and lash out with guns or fists. If an enemy was trying to find you, such noise would give away your position.

Tilman opened his eyes, lay unmoving, listening, looking, senses coming alive. A waning quarter moon crested the mountains to the east, casting pale light across the small hill. He heard nothing, and saw Butter watching the desert to his front. Tilman sat up, moved soundlessly to Butter's side. Butter exhaled softly, put his mouth near Tilman's ear and whispered, "Left front, maybe ten yards out . . . at least one."

Tilman nodded; reached for one of the Colt pistols he'd cocked and laid on a rock nearby before going to sleep. Normally the piece held five cartridges, with the hammer resting on an empty chamber, but he'd put a sixth round in both his belt guns because the work he expected this night called for quick movement at close quarters, with only the small movement of a thumb to cock the weapon after firing it. Life depended on speed, gut reaction without thought if it came to a hand-to-hand fight, and it seemed that was sure to happen soon.

Butter held a pistol in one hand and a large knife in another, and like a stalking panther about to spring he was still, tense and unmoving with concentration. Near a small rock a shadow appeared where none had been a moment before and Butter shot, red fire from the muzzle flashing with a flat "BAM!" followed almost immediately by a grunted "Unn-h," from the shadows and a scurry of movement.

The Apaches were coming. They'd be more careful now they knew the white men were alert. Butter hit the first one, but couldn't tell how badly the Indian was wounded. Tilman scanned his surroundings, careful not to stare at an object but rather to look alongside what he wanted to see, for a man's eyes play tricks on him in the night. If a man stares at a bush or a rock at night before long he will swear it's moving, has taken on a man's shape, is coming for him, and while concentrating on the false enemy leaves himself open to attack from the real enemy approaching stealthily. A man has to stay alert, calm, and keep his wits. It's the difference between living and dying.

Rustling sounds, from somewhere out front, and an odd whirring overhead and then behind, and a surprised cry, "Hoah!" It was Smith. "An arrow, almost got me!" he said, relief in his voice, "Heads up, boys."

An Apache had fired an arrow nearly straight up, and the arrow dug itself into the earth beside Smith, giving him a start. Soon several more fell, but none as close as the first. The men scrunched down low, trying to make themselves as small a target for falling arrows as possible. Quiet settled over the small hill. The Apaches had tried to get close from the front, had tried shooting arrows into the tiny perimeter. What would they try next? Would they give up?

The moon rose higher in the cold night sky, offering more light; the Big Dipper made its way across the blackness, circling a brilliantly flashing North Star as morning approached. A sudden scuffling noise came from behind Tilman and Butter, grunts, muffled curses, a cry of pain followed by a brief whistling sound and a thud. Then, Tilman heard heavy breathing; someone muttering quiet words . . . in English.

"OK over there?" Tilman whispered hoarsely.

"OK," came a breathless response from one of the black troopers. "Two of 'em rushed us but we's taken care of 'em." After a pause, "Broke my shovel, though."

A nervous chuckle came from the other trooper, "The Army'll make you pay for it, I bet."

A mumbled admonition was followed by, "Aw, they already know where we are!"

Tilman smiled grimly. Good men. They find humor in the worst situations, and that's what will keep them sane.

The pre-dawn twilight transformed the world from black to shades of gray, devoid of color and not yet warmed by the sun. Butter, shivering from the chill in the air, raised his head to look around, blowing on his cold hands to warm them. "They're pullin' back, I seen movement yonder, in them rocks, maybe quarter of a mile—you see?"

Stiffly, Tilman made his way to the Gatling, called for the loader, and fired a wake-up twenty-round burst at the Apaches, the sound ripping obscenely through the morning silence, echoing from the mesa. A cloud of powder smoke drifted slowly away. "Good morning, Texas!" he shouted defiantly.

Butter let loose the screeching, spine-tingling howl of a Rebel yell, coughed, hawked and spat, and laughed aloud. "Boys, I need some coffee to warm my voice box!"

"And let's put a little something in it to ease the stiffness in my shoulder," added Leoni, sitting upright, but with his right arm bound tightly to his side to immobilize it. "Somebody get my flask." The man had passed out when Tilman probed his wound and dusted it with ground chaparral leaves. After a restless night of tossing and turning in his blankets, Leoni was surprisingly alert in spite of his wound.

"Better make that just plain water," Tilman suggested, tossing him a canteen.

Burney stood beside Tilman at the gun. "I didn't expect to hit anything, just wanted to let those Apaches know there's still plenty of fight left in us," Tilman said. "Besides, it makes everyone feel better after a long night."

"Get another magazine." Burney spoke in a croaking whisper to the loader as he gingerly felt his painfully swollen neck. "I owe them."

Chapter Twenty-three

Since dawn Maddie and Lomida had followed Diosune through the canyon to pick herbs near the river below the encampment. The days were getting cooler and the air was brisk with the promise of the first snows of the winter. The empty trees were bare of leaves and the scrubby grass was brown. Many of the birds had migrated to a warmer area further south in Mexico for the winter months. The plants Diosune searched for were also harder to find.

As they made their way down the canyon, the sounds of distant gunfire came on the wind, a steady and continuous but faint popping. "Listen! I've heard that sound before," Lomida whispered to Maddie. "That's the sound of one of those funny looking guns at the fort."

"I'll bet it's the soldiers from the fort, and they're looking for us," Maddie answered, reassuring Lomida as well as bolstering her own sense of hope.

The wind shifted around to come from the south, and they heard no more of the gunfire.

Their search took most of the day and the three were finally on the way home when they detected the sound of a lone rider coming up the trail to the hideout. Maddie and Lomida moved behind Diosune and they all hid in a clump of reeds that grew thick along the river.

Comes From War passed by on his horse, his long coal-black hair flying behind him. A magnificent looking warrior who was used to taking what he wanted, the man moved as one with his horse. Maddie couldn't help but shudder. Why had he come back without the others? She could think of only one reason. Luis had threatened all the men to leave her alone, Chuy's orders. But, if Luis and Chuy weren't here, how would they know what happened?

Diosune, apparently having no more trust in Comes From War than Maddie, motioned for the two girls to be quiet with a finger to her lips. The three remained hidden as the man disappeared from view up the trail. It was only a matter of time before he came for Maddie, and there would be only a lame girl and an old woman to protect her. No, she would not stand behind Lomida or Diosune for protection, but . . . what could she do? How would she protect herself?

Cautiously the group made their way back to shelter, Diosune leading them to camp from a different direction and into the hut without being seen. She motioned for Maddie and Lomida to stay put and left them alone. Soon Maddie, peeking through a gap between the sticks of the hut's walls, saw Comes From War and Diosune at the front of the cave. She could hear much talking between the two and the pop of a jug being uncorked. Then Diosune was laughing while passing a bottle to Comes From War. The man grunted words Maddie could not understand, then upended the bottle, swallowing a long drink. He cleared his throat, took another drink, and then began grumbling at Diosune. Maddie heard the word *cigarro,* and Diosune went bustling off for tobacco, her laugh a dry cackle in the cave's interior.

What was the woman up to? Maddie tried to sidle up to the window to listen but they were speaking very rapid Spanish and Maddie could make out only a few words. Something about *esta noche* and *mas tequila.* Maddie could only guess that Diosune was trying to get Comes From War drunk, but why would she do that? An evil, willful man could only become an evil, uncontrollable drunk.

Hardly an hour passed before the sky was dark and cold winds came gusting through the canyon. Outside the hut no more than a faint blue light came from the stars making it almost impossible to see, for moonrise was still hours away. From close by came the sound of a thud. Soon Diosune came, one hand cupped protectively around the flame of a lighted candle, and entered the room. "Quickly. *Rápidamente.*" Diosune motioned for the girls to get their shawls. She poured water from the *olla* onto the dirt floor, and mixed a muddy paste. "Excuse me," and she smeared it on their faces and hands so they were not recognizable as white women.

"Diosune!" Maddie thought she had gone crazy, *"Está usted loco?"*

Diosune shushed them and handed them each a heavy U.S. Cavalry canteen full of water and a kerchief containing tortillas and jerked meat of indeterminate nature. Maddie didn't ask.

Diosune went to a jar she had been working with for the last few days. It held acorns from an oak motte located in the dry hills above the camp. They had been soaked and boiled down to thick brownish water. Taking a comb she sat Maddie down and combed the mixture into her hair and then did the same to Lomida. Once finished the two were amazed to find themselves transformed into brown-haired, or rather, butternut-haired women. The dye had a slight woody smell and Maddie tried not to think about what they looked like, just being glad for once there was no mirror.

"Oh, Miss Maddie. I don't think Comes From War would want you now." The young girl bravely joked.

"Watch yourself, little lady," Maddie tried to joke along with her. She had no idea what Diosune had in mind but she knew the woman was a friend and Maddie trusted her with their lives.

"Ssshh." The girls quietly took small bundles of their meager belongings and the three left the shack, passing by the cave opening.

"Uugh." By the dim light of a single fat lamp they saw Comes From War, sprawled on the rocky floor by an upended table. He had vomited on himself and wallowed in the mess. Suddenly he groaned, sat up, and the three froze in their tracks. Muttering, smacking his lips, he swept unseeing eyes in their direction, flopped loosely down and was out once more, stone-cold drunk from Diosune's concoction of tequila laced with some odd little mushrooms and herbs she had gathered during the day.

Although it was now after midnight the two girls followed Diosune in the soft light of a quarter moon as she made her way down the familiar trail, passing wraith-like from darkly shadowed places into the light and back to the shadows again.

Chapter Twenty-four

Daylight found Diosune, Maddie and Lomida tired but safe at the mouth of the canyon. When they stopped for a drink of water and a bite of cold tortilla, Diosune showed a paper to Maddie. It seemed to be a map of sorts. Diosune pointed to one side, "Here." She pointed to a line on the picture. "This place we are." She looked out across the valley and pointed with her crooked finger to a dry stream bed that came down to the river from the north, said the word *"terlingua,"* and pointed again to the map. The creek she pointed to was the line on the map, Terlingua Creek. "You go here." She continued to trace a route along the line on the map. "Walk by *terlingua abaja*." Pointing to a low hill some miles distant, she said, "You go." She pointed as she quickly spoke. "Pepe, *mi hermano,* he will help you. He has many sheep." She then placed a small cross from around her neck in Maddie's hand. "Show *cruz.* He know from Diosune."

Then Diosune pushed her way through a clump of

reeds and returned with a small burro that someone had tied among some rocks. She turned once more to Maddie. "Comes From War *muy malo*. He hurt you." She went to Lomida and lifted her onto the little burro. Giving Lomida the food and the canteens of water to carry she patted her hand and gave the burro a push. Diosune turned once more to Maddie. "You go now. Follow Terlingua." She touched Maddie on the shoulder, and made the sign of the cross. "*Vaya con Dios.*"

"But Diosune." Maddie realized the danger the woman now faced for helping her to escape.

"I go *mi familia* now." Diosune pointed to rugged mountains across the valley, sharply outlined by the rising sun in the east. "Chisos my home." The old woman was soon lost to sight as she followed her own path.

The burro seemed to know the way up the creek bed so Maddie had no choice but to follow. Behind her from the canyon she thought she heard a distant voice, raised in impotent rage, and knew that Comes From War awakened to find his prize had flown. Maybe she only imagined the voice. Maybe it was the wind playing tricks on her mind. "Now I know I'm going crazy." She mumbled. "We're hours away from camp." Still, she had no doubt that Comes From War would not be happy when he discovered them missing and would find them if he could. She must get the two of them to safety, the sooner the better. She hoped that Diosune had put plenty of herbs in that tequila and that Comes From War slept a long time.

Cuchillo Negro held up his hand, signaling a halt. "Leave the men here. Come. We will look and see where the white men fought the Apaches."

Chuy and Luis dismounted in the cold, stark early morning light. Leaving their force of fighting men, now numbering twenty-eight because of those who had come from the Sierra del Carmen camp to join Chuy in Lajitas, the two men followed Cuchillo Negro to a vantage point. Squinting into the morning sun, they saw an Indian camp, perhaps half a mile distant, smoke from cooking fires rising vertically in the still air. A few Apaches could be seen walking in the camp, and near it there was a herd of perhaps thirty horses.

Cuchillo Negro pointed into the distance, past the Indian camp. "And over there is the hill where the white men are."

Chuy called to one of his men who quickly brought a small hand telescope. Chuy studied the hill. "I see them. They make coffee. Two black white soldiers, no, three, and four whites." After a moment, he said, "Two of the white men have been wounded and wear bandages." Then gleefully, "They have my gun! I see her there! Magnificent!" He laughed like a child getting his most cherished toy at Christmas, then passed the telescope to Luis, "See!"

"How many Apaches?" Chuy asked.

Shifting the telescope, Luis studied the Indian camp for a moment. "I see eighteen."

"We will make them pay, and after we have saved"— he paused to smile—"yes, *saved* the white men, we will take the gun from them, a gift showing their gratitude to us for saving them from those savages! And then we will kill them where they stand!"

After a final look at the ground before them, Chuy and Luis agreed on the best tactics to surprise and overwhelm the Apaches. Dividing his forces, Chuy rode in front of one column, Luis the other, and they made their way down the mountain to open the battle. The men were eager, for after all, this was their life.

"Somethin' goin' on!" one of the troopers cried, leaping to his feet for a better view, pointing at the clouds of dust rising behind the Indians. Sounds of gunfire, heavy at first and then intermittent, rolled across the valley.

Tilman stood, as did everyone except the hard-hit Leoni. Burney lifted his binoculars and after a moment whispered, "Two columns are hitting the Apaches, one from their rear, and one from the south flank." He paused to swallow, his neck and throat sore. "Whoever they are, they're not our Army."

"Until we find out who those people are, let's be careful," Tilman ordered. "Check your guns and lay out extra cartridges. Get the spare magazines for the Gatling ready, and finish building your breastworks around it. We could be in for another fight."

After only a few minutes the Apaches could be seen riding hard to the north, hotly pursued by some of their attackers. Most of the mounted men did not pursue the Apaches, but regrouped and turned to advance toward the knoll. Tilman estimated the number of men arranged in a loose column behind two men, who had to be their leaders, to be about thirty horsemen. They came on at a trot toward the knoll. Unsure of their intentions, Tilman hesitated until they were about a hundred yards distant. He could clearly see by their dress and distinctive wide-brimmed sombreros that the men were Mexicans and they were well armed. "That's close enough!" Tilman shouted. When the men kept coming, Tilman threw his rifle to his shoulder and taking quick aim, fired at the well-dressed leader, the one with the clean white shirt and shining silver *conchos* on his trousers.

"*Ayee!*" Luis shouted, surprised as a bullet knocked the hat from his head to dangle behind him on the stampede string.

"*Alto!*" Chuy shouted, raising his hand to stop the men riding behind, bringing the mass to a nervous, threatening halt about seventy-five yards from the knoll. Luis looked at the hole in his hat, reached up and tentatively felt his head, relieved that he had not been hit. When he brought his hand down, there was hair on it. The bullet had cut a swath through his hair, his pride.

"Look!" Luis said in a concerned voice, showing the hair to Chuy. "Think of all the women who almost put on mourning clothes today!"

"Hey, *gringo!*" Chuy shouted, "Why you shoot at me?"

Several of the horsemen began to drift around to the sides, as if to flank the hill.

"If I'd shot at *you* I'd be talkin' to the dandy right now," Tilman shouted. "Tell those men to stay where they are!"

"That 'un you shot at," Butter said, "that's Luis Valenzuela!"

"So it is," Tilman answered, "and he don't look too happy."

At a word from Chuy, the riders moved back. "You bring the gun here to exchange for the white woman and the girl, yes?"

"Are they all right?"

"Sure. You think we hurt them?"

"Where are they?"

"They are safe. You give us the gun, we bring them to you."

"No!" Tilman countered. "You bring them to us and when we see they're all right, you get the gun."

"Cuidado, gringo"—Chuy was becoming agitated—"you don't tell Chuy Ayala what to do!"

Tilman watched as Luis began an animated conversation with the man who called himself Chuy Ayala. The riders exchanged glances, tensed.

"Hey, hey," Butter muttered, "look out!"

Luis dug spurs into his mount and led half the men into a run to Tilman's left, while Chuy led the remainder straight at Tilman, who knelt behind a boulder and brought his Winchester into play. Behind him the Gatling opened with a deafening roar as the gunner raked the line of onrushing riders, knocking men and horses screaming, kicking to the ground. The charge became a frantic retreat.

To the left Burney, Smith, and Leoni were firing pistols into the second group which was almost upon them, while Butter worked his Winchester as fast as he could. The troopers on the Gatling muscled the awkward weapon to bear on the new threat, for it had only a limited traverse angle, and began firing, again sending the riders into a frenzy of fear as they attempted to escape with their lives.

"Keep firing!" Burney's hoarse whisper came in the sudden silence. "Don't let 'em get away."

The gunners continued to crank the Gatling with deadly effect, knocking down three other horses; only one rider regained his feet to struggle to cover. When the noise of battle quieted, Tilman shook his head, his ears ringing again.

He could make out Luis and Chuy riding off out of sight, the remainder of their men straggling behind them.

"Think they've gone to get the girls, Tilman?"

"Wish I did but I think they have gone for more men. What do you reckon?"

"I agree with you, pard."

Tilman nodded and kept an eye as Butter disappeared behind him for a moment.

"Coffee?"

Tilman gratefully accepted a steaming cup of coffee from a grim Butter.

"I've had better," Tilman allowed, sipping the hot brew gingerly.

"An' you've had worse!" Butter shot back.

The hard-packed gravel was unmarked by their passage as Maddie led the way into the bed of Terlingua Creek, dry now that the season of little rain was upon them, but hidden from view by thick brush and scrubby mesquite hardy enough to sink roots deep into the soil to find moisture. The creek bed was filled with gravel, loose cobbles, and small boulders. They had to trust the sure-footed burro. Their route took them gradually uphill, and the going was slow.

Soon after they started, the pop of gunfire came from the west, rose to a steady noise where individual shots were no longer distinguishable, along with men's voices shouting, screaming in anger and pain. Looking in the direction of the sound, Maddie saw a cloud of smoke, or dust, rising into the sky. Maddie had no idea what that battle was about.

"Miss Maddie. Listen. Do you hear gunshots? Are the bandits coming for us?"

"Shh. Lomida. If anything, that's help coming for us."

Were the Indians attacking the soldiers sent to rescue them? What would become of them if the Indians killed all the soldiers? "We don't have the time or the strength to go see what's happening. Diosune says at her brother's we'll be safe and I believe her. Let's keep on this direction." Maddie knew there was no time to waste. Diosune promised safety with her brother, and that was Maddie's goal. The shooting stopped after a short time, and by mid-morning all was quiet, the only sounds their own.

Undernourished, they stopped frequently to rest. The girls were dismayed to find their journey led through a harsh land filled with things that scratched, stabbed, and tore at their skin through their clothes, and crawling things with stingers, ugly lizards and black, hairy, tarantula spiders, but worst were the inch-long and razor-sharp thorns on the mesquite.

"My face. Is it getting red, Maddie?" Lomida tried to pull the shawl over her face a little more. The heat of the sun was intense for there was little breeze to cool them. They had been in and out of the little shade of the scrubby trees along the stream, and the unforgiving sun drew moisture from their thin bodies, their perspiration evaporating without cooling them.

Maddie put a finger in a small pouch that Diosune had given her and scooped some of the aloe vera plant mixture to smear it on Lomida. A thin shawl protected her but her fair skin was dry and freckled and her lips were cracking. Maddie felt Lomida's forehead and it was warmer than it should be. Occasionally, a light wind rustled the brush above them, but they saw no other human being.

Maddie had no sense of distance and she could not guess that the mountain Diosune pointed to as their destination was as yet nearly two miles away. An iron will kept her moving, pulling, pushing, swatting the little burro, keeping a weary Lomida from falling, ever climbing, unaware that the sun was near it's zenith in the sky. The hill seemed hardly closer and seemed somehow to taunt her.

"How many?" Chuy raged.

"Seven dead, eleven wounded or injured, and three more lost their horses," Luis explained, "and four ran away."

"I will go to Lajitas. We must have more men. We must attack from all sides. Luis, you go for the woman and the girl. The *gringos* will not fire upon the girl," Chuy said. "Send Agapito to me, and tell him to bring his long rifle."

"*Sí, mi Jefe.*" Luis answered, glad to have reason to be away from this place of death.

Chapter Twenty-five

"Lomida, do you see the other water canteen. I can't find it." Maddie frantically hunted through their meager belongings searching for the precious liquid.

"No, Miss Maddie. Wasn't it behind me? That is where we put both canteens I thought." The two girls rearranged everything only to discover that their water was gone. Apparently one of the canteens had been lost along the way.

Maddie's tongue felt huge in her mouth. She struggled to put one foot in front of the other. Lomida cried softly, but no tears came. "I am so thirsty." The day drew on, a day without end.

"Look, Miss Maddie," Lomida whispered, "there's a hut."

Tears came to Maddie's eyes as she looked at a small ramshackle stone and reed building. Incredibly, she had made it. *They* had made it.

"Is that the man we're supposed to see?" Lomida whispered.

A few hundred yards away a man stood among a flock of sheep near the hut, watching their progress, alert for danger. A dog and a little boy urged the sheep toward a small corral. Two horses watched from a second corral, curious, ears alert.

Could the man be Pepe? Leaving Lomida and the burro, Maddie cautiously approached and held out the small cross Diosune had given her. Maddie placed it in his hands and the man's eyes widened with recognition as he slowly turned the cross over in his hands and then said, "Diosune." He put the cross around his neck and waited.

"Help us?" Maddie said. She pointed to Lomida. "Please, *senor*, she needs rest and out of the sun."

"*Sí, senorita,*" the man said, and switching to English, continued. "You are from my sister. Come, we have water and food, and a place to rest away from the sun."

The young man named Agapito carried a captured U.S. Army Springfield rifle, Model 1873. The heavy, single-shot, breech-loading rifle chambered a .45–.70 cartridge and in the hands of a good shooter was accurate up to one thousand yards. Pito had to be the best shot for miles around, and Chuy wanted him to try to take care of those white soldiers. A slim nineteen year old, Pito stood four inches over five feet tall, had the keen eyes of an eagle, and a sure judgment of distances over open ground; zealously he believed that Chuy Ayala was a man of vision, a man to respect. It was an honor for Agapito to ride with him.

Agapito dressed in dull gray and brown colors, not

because he was shy or uncaring of his appearance, but because he had studied the predators of the desert, noted their colors, and wanted to blend in with his surroundings as they did. Unseen, he would strike and steal away. Taking a canteen and a few tortillas along with a bag of cartridges, the young man made his way into the valley. He searched for, and near noon, found a satisfactory place he estimated to be about nine hundred yards from the little knoll where the white men lay. Now he would watch, and when the time was right, begin to kill them one by one.

"Useless," the gunner reported. "One of the barrels busted wide open, bent the two beside it out of true. We can't fix it."

"What about Trooper Lee?" Leoni asked, for the loader had taken some metal shards in his hands when the barrel burst.

"He be okay. You know two of the mules for the gun is dead, and two hosses, right?"

Before Leoni could answer, he was interrupted by the scout.

"Throw me one of those canteens," Smith said as he stood up to stretch, "I'm awful—" With a whack a bullet struck the scout and he was bowled over backwards, dead where he fell. The sound of a distant shot came immediately, and the men saw a puff of gun smoke half a mile away, fading as they watched.

"Take cover!" Leoni shouted as the men scrambled to get behind their breastworks of rock. No one had to look twice to see that Smith was beyond help.

"Uh-oh," Butter said with a knowing look at Tilman,

"they got 'em a long shooter out there." Another puff of smoke bloomed and another slug zinged overhead, followed by the sound of the shot.

"He's in those rocks," Tilman said, thumbing up the peep sight and sighting down the barrel of his heavy Winchester '76. "And this time things are a whole lot different. How far would you say, Butter?"

"Near three-quarters of a mile, I reckon"—Butter squinted into the distance—"a touch less, mebbe." After studying the distance, Butter suggested, "Hold off a tad to the right, for I 'spect there's some wind out yonder."

"Wind's light, but I'll put some Kentucky windage on it. Maybe I can give him one back," Tilman said, his voice trailing off with concentration before he fired.

The afternoon became a deadly private duel of carefully aimed shots between Tilman and Agapito. Neither could gain an advantage. Agapito shifted his position. Tilman did the same, the men stalking each other across hundreds of yards of open space, often not knowing where the enemy was until he fired. Late in the day Tilman gave up in frustration, for the sun was setting and, because of the glare when looking westward, he could no longer see where his opponent waited. Tilman knew that whoever the man was, if Tilman raised his head, the sun would illuminate his face to make a perfect target and it would be over. Stalemate. They were pinned down, unable to move. Besides, the wounded couldn't ride very far, even if they had enough horses.

During the night, while Tilman and Butter kept watch, the soldiers buried Smith in a dry stream bed near the knoll. Burney spoke a few words over the grave, and then the men returned to the hill in the darkness. The soldiers arranged themselves as comfortably as they could and tried to get some sleep while Tilman and Butter took the first watch. Leoni slept fitfully, mumbling in his native language.

"What's your plan?" Butter asked quietly.

"My plan? We never made it close enough to John's daughter and the teacher to even *start* to plan," Tilman said, tiredly.

"I don't mean for them," Butter said, "I mean for us."

Maddie and Lomida slept for several hours until Pepe woke them. The afternoon sun was low on the horizon and soon it would be cold as the day's heat would evaporate as fast as the light of day. "*Senorita*, here. Eat, *por favor*." He handed her a bowl of steaming hot beans and warm tortillas. Maddie found the fresh, hot tortillas were hard to beat. The best restaurant in the world would be pressed to beat their taste.

"*Gracias*, Pepe. They are good and I am so hungry." Maddie brushed a stray lock of hair from her face and smiled at Pepe. He blushed.

Lomida sat up to eat and took a tortilla. "I'm not very hungry, Miss Maddie. I'm sorry."

Maddie set down the beans, looked closely at Lomida. What she saw wasn't good. The young girl had been through a lot and hadn't complained but it was catching up with her. The face that peered back at Maddie was red and flushed. A quick touch of her hand on Lomida's forehead told her that Lomida was burning up with fever.

Pepe also noticed and left quickly, returning with a cloth that was dripping with cool water. Maddie took it, nodded thanks, and laid it across Lomida's brow. She needed to see a doctor and they were in the middle of nowhere.

Pepe motioned for her to bring her food and come outside with him. While she ate, he introduced her to a young herdsman named Salvador. "Salvador is a good boy. He will take you to the mission at Lajitas. There we learn our English," Pepe explained proudly. "The sisters are good people. They help all who come to them. They will help the child."

Salvador nodded agreement and shyly looked up at Maddie before quickly turning his eyes away. He had never seen a woman he thought so beautiful, and he blushed every time he looked at her. He had brought the two horses she had seen earlier, with sheepskins for saddles, Indian style. The bridles were old and had been patched with rawhide strips.

Maddie sopped the last of her beans with a piece of tortilla. "I didn't know beans could taste so good." She hadn't realized she was so hungry.

Pepe continued. "You and Lomida need to go before *el noche*, the night, comes. Much danger, too dark." He went in with Maddie and helped her get Lomida and their few belongings. Outside, Maddie pulled herself onto the back of one of the horses. Salvador climbed aboard the other horse, and Pepe handed Lomida up to Maddie.

"Thank you." Maddie waved as the two horses started toward Lajitas. "Tell Diosune *gracias* too." The horses picked up their pace and Pepe soon became a small dot on the brown landscape.

Conversation was impossible as Salvador rode ahead, checking the route to make sure they were safe, careful with the great responsibility now on his shoulders. He, Salvador, had to deliver the beautiful woman and the girl to the mission. "Not far," he said to Maddie.

Drifting in and out of an exhausted sleep the feverish Lomida was a full-time job for Maddie while the horses made their way across the prairie. Sometimes Lomida would shiver, than sweat, than slump. Maddie held her close.

Chapter Twenty-six

Daylight was almost gone when Salvador pointed to a scattering of stone, mud and reed huts and clusters of more substantial adobe buildings, and said "Lajitas." The village, perched on a bluff overlooking the Rio Grande, was settling for the coming night. Smoke from cooking fires hung in the still air. Maddie saw that a road of sorts led down to a river fording place.

Salvador wanted to impress Maddie with his worldly knowledge. He explained, "Lajitas means 'little flat rocks,' for there are many such stones near the village. You see some of the people stack them for small buildings."

They rode past a large adobe structure on the village outskirts overlooking the river. Maddie saw that it was a cantina, dimly lit by candles on some of the tables; someone inside was strumming a guitar. A man's placating voice came from the deep shadows, answered by a woman's angry shout, followed by a short, bitter laugh. The horses seemed to know where they were going and made their way along the trail until reaching a small mission.

Salvador got off his horse, and quickly came to help Maddie with Lomida. Lomida slid into Salvador's waiting arms and he carried her into the mission gates. Maddie slowly got down from her horse and winced in pain as her feet touched the ground. Both feet were bruised and blistered, her ankles ached and her knees were stiff from walking the uneven, rocky stream bed. She was exhausted, the little sleep she'd managed during the afternoon had been good, but her body cried out for more. She touched her face, amazed to feel remnants of her mud mask still in place. When she had time she'd rub more aloe and mud paste on herself and Lomida, but for the time being she would just have to walk gingerly, wishing she had Indian Annie's soft moccasins to wear.

An elderly priest was getting ready to close the main entrance doors at the front of a low wall surrounding the mission when he saw Maddie, Lomida and Salvador.

"Quien es?" the old man asked.

Salvador quickly identified himself to the priest, and after a moment's conversation, the priest turned and called to someone behind him. Several nuns hurried out to surround Salvador and Lomida, making concerned noises, speaking in a mixture of Spanish, English, and something else that Maddie didn't identify.

In a matter of minutes, Maddie and Lomida were in a small room where a nun, who introduced herself as Sister Serifina, quickly assumed charge and called out several orders to the others and proceeded to take care of Lomida.

"Gracias, Salvador. Thank you so much." Salvador

smiled, disappeared into the main part of the mission, and it was quiet except for Sister Serifina.

"How long?"

"I beg your pardon?"

"How long ill?" Sister Serifina pointed to Lomida.

"Oh. Her fever. Since yesterday." Words came in a torrent as Maddie, relieved to have a sympathetic listener, began telling Sister Serifina what had transpired the last few weeks, when the sister held up her hand.

"We know who you are," Sister Serifina spoke quietly. "The people saw when you were brought in by the Apaches and watched as you left with one of Chuy's men, and they told us. But we were afraid you were lost in Mexico. You must tell us where you were and of your escape, but after you have rested."

The other women and the priest entered the room and were all making concerned sounds in different languages.

"Oh, you poor thing."

"Mi pobricita."

"Comment l'avez-vous tenu?"

"Is that French? You speak French?" Maddie was confused.

"But of course. I am French." The young sister beside Maddie smiled at her confusion. "We are from France, Sister Theresa and myself are from France." The young sister smiled and pointed to another older woman who had moved to help Sister Serifina. "Sister Serifina and Sister Marie are from Mexico, and Father Lonigan is from Boston in Massachusetts."

"But how . . . ?"

"God sent us here. Who knows, maybe he sent us to help you." The young woman laughed and glided away.

Maddie thought she must be on wheels under that long skirt.

"Maddie . . ."

"Shhh, Lomida. It is okay. The sisters will help us now. Don't worry, little one." Maddie stood by Lomida's side holding her hand. She had become very fond of this child. She would miss her when she left to live in El Paso.

Sister Serifina motioned for Maddie to move so she could give Lomida some broth. Maddie nodded and left the room to step outside, for the closed-in room felt strangely confining. The courtyard was quiet as the first stars twinkled in the clear evening sky. Maddie heard nothing but the sound of peace and quiet. She walked stiffly around the yard, coming to stop at a small chapel. She pulled open the darkly weathered wooden door and inside by the light of several candles were rows of worn but sturdy benches and hand-carved, brightly painted figures of saints. Two of the sisters knelt near the front for evening prayer. Arising, they stopped at a wrought-iron rack by the altar. There were rows of small candles in short, red glass jars, and they each lit one of the candles. They nodded and without a word left through a side door. Maddie looked around and realized she was alone in the chapel. It had been a long time since she had said a prayer, probably not since her parents had died. But the chapel seemed to give her a sense of understanding and Maddie sat in the near darkness and solitude. She prayed for Lomida and the men from Fort Davis who came to rescue them, and for Pepe, Salvador and for Diosune, who had risked their lives for the two hostages, strangers until a few short days, even hours ago. Suddenly tears of relief were streaming down her face. Drying her eyes on her sleeve, she got up and went to the front of the chapel, lighting one of the candles as she had seen the sisters do. For the first time in years Madeline Brown felt at peace. In the middle of a battle no less. Life was strange.

Chapter Twenty-seven

"Gentlemen," Sol Burney rasped, "I believe it's time for a council of war."

Tilman could hardly see the young officer in the last light of the day, so he moved nearer. Butter had been talking with the black troopers on the reverse slope, so he came to listen. Leoni, his shoulder stiff and sore but no longer bleeding, leaned against a rock beside Burney.

"Here's how I see it. There are just the five of us. I'm shot, Sergeant Leoni's shot. The Gatling is ruined, and we've been pinned down on this hill most of the day." Burney paused to clear his throat and take a sip of water. "We don't know how many of those people are out there or even if they'll still be there after sunset. We know they have a long shooter." Hearing no comments, he continued. "I don't want to simply sit here and wait for them to come and take us. We need to know some answers so we can decide what to do. Somebody has to go out there, but my troopers are too green; they've never done this before. Mr. Wagner?"

"I've done things like this before. I'll go," Butter said.

"No offense, Butter," Burney said, "but I believe Tilman is the best one for a job like this."

"All right, listen carefully," Tilman said. "There's a crescent moon coming up about an hour before dawn, but I'll be back before then. We don't know if they're coming for us tonight, so be on the lookout and don't shoot me!"

"I'll take the last watch," Butter offered, "you can count on me."

Tilman opened his saddlebags and got out the moccasins he always carried and a Bowie knife John Law had given him before he left the post; he removed his hat, vest, and his boots and slipped into the soft leathers. Tilman shucked the gun belt, took the .45 and stuck it in his belt. When he was ready he touched Butter's shoulder and without a word slipped into the darkness. Guided by the stars Tilman slowly worked his way through the night toward his enemy. In the distance a match flared, held a moment, winked out. The red dot of a cigarette glowed, a pinpoint beacon in the darkness. The glow brightened as a man drew smoke, and faded again. Smoking in the open at night revealed a sign of poorly disciplined men, and a dead giveaway of a position. The smoker's night vision was ruined for at least a half an hour, an advantage for Tilman. After a bit the smoker finished, the glow extinguished.

Tilman placed each moccasined foot carefully, noiselessly touching his foot to the ground before he shifted his weight forward, for in the quiet of the desert night a wrong step and a snapping twig or the sound of a tumbling stone could bring a bullet. It was tense, nerve-wracking work. The sound of a thorn ripping cloth, or even a branch brushing against a man's jeans could alert an enemy. Young man's work, Tilman thought as he made his way through the night. His senses strained for any danger. How long had he been moving? Was he at last getting close to the Mexicans?

There, a sound. He froze. His hearing didn't seem as good as it once was, for his ears still rang from Bill Ward's pistol shot back in Colorado, lately made worse by the Gatling firing over his head. The sound came again. A man snoring! Now he knew he was close.

Under the pale light of a waning crescent moon in the pre-dawn chill Tilman, safely back from his reconnaissance, pulled off the moccasins and put them away. Soon he was fully dressed again, went to the water keg and tipped it to drink deeply. Blowing on his hands to warm them, he came and sat by Butter. Butter said nothing to break the silence, waiting until the stress and tension of the night's work left Tilman. Across the desert, a flicker of fire light became visible, grew and danced on some rocks marking the position of the Mexican gunmen. Voices, faint with distance, were raised in emphatic consternation.

"Lemme make us some coffee," Butter suggested, "seeing as how them fellers over there is up an' about."

"Lieutenant," Tilman said quietly, "we have to talk."

Soon cups of steaming black coffee, strong and bitter as Butter always made it, were passed around, the men holding the cups with both hands to savor the warmth on stiff fingers.

"There were seven in the camp last night," Tilman

said, "but maybe more if I didn't see all of 'em. I managed to cut loose their ponies and run them off."

"That's what all the ruckus was about a while ago," Butter said. "They woke up an' found themselves afoot!"

"This is fair coffee. Least I can't see the bottom of the cup," Tilman said to Butter. "How about another?" Turning to Burney, Tilman continued, "Well, we need to get moving or else . . ."

A bullet smacked viciously into a rock and whined into the morning sky. The sound of a shot came across the desert.

"Down!" Butter said. "Reckon you should have tried to find that shooter while you was out there! Feller's *good*."

"Lieutenant, we're going to have to ride out of here," Tilman said.

A horse screamed and fell as another shot boomed.

"Get them horses behind cover!" Butter yelled as the troopers scrambled to move the animals into defilade.

"Put some fire out there," Leoni called to the troopers, "keep 'em ducking."

"Lieutenant, tomorrow morning before first light we're gonna ride," Tilman said over the answering fire from the troopers, "or we'll die here on this hill."

Chapter Twenty-eight

Maddie moved from the bright sunlight into the shade under a covered walkway in front of the mission office not far from the gate. She had been to draw water from the well to help the sisters when she had seen two mounted men riding at breakneck speed toward the mission. With a growing sense of dread she stood in the shadows behind an archway and pulled a worn shawl over her hair to partially hide her face. She had kept the brown color on her hair, but she knew she would be easy to recognize if anybody looked closely.

"Miss Maddie."

Maddie jumped as Salvador gently guided her further back into the shadows. Salvador's dark eyes peered out from his wide brimmed straw hat. "I was by the gate keeping watch when I saw two men coming here from Lajitas."

Maddie and Salvador kept out of sight as the riders jumped their horses across the low courtyard wall which ran around the mission, sending a flock of chickens flying, and reined to a stop not ten feet in front of where they stood. The priest, summoned by the disturbance, came from the office to find out who the men were and what they wanted.

"That man," Salvador whispered, "he rides with El Chamuscado."

The riders dismounted from their horses and began to talk rapidly in Spanish. The priest held up his hands, palms outward, motioning for the men to speak slowly. Maddie couldn't follow the talk but she realized that Salvador was deep in concentration as he motioned for her to be quiet so he could listen. With a flurry of angry hand movements, stomping and posturing and rapid speech the two men turned from the priest to enter the main mission.

"Miss, they ask, who are the two riders who come to the mission last night," Salvador interpreted. "In the village there is talk of strangers here. Priest say many *gringos* have passed by here but people often come through the mission on their way to other places so who knows where they are today."

Maddie could hardly breathe. "Salvador. That is Luis Valenzuela, and the other is . . ."

"Who, Miss Maddie?"

"The other man is Comes From War. He is very bad, Salvador. He is why Diosune helped us escape." Maddie's heart rose in her throat with the realization that Luis knew of her escape, and with Comes From War's help both men were looking for her.

"Do not be afraid, Miss Maddie. That man, he does not know you are here. The good father and the sisters will not lie; only maybe not speak all the truth."

Salvador smiled. "Maybe their Spanish will be bad, and they misunderstand." He shrugged. "Who knows?"

Maddie fought to control a sinking feeling as Salvador talked. The boy hadn't said ten words all yesterday and now he was a wealth of information. "What do we do now, Salvador?"

"You stay here. They will not look for you with the old women who weave baskets." He pointed to a small group of women from the village sitting in the shade against the wall, working on colorful baskets that the mission sold or traded to make ends meet and provide food for the needy in the community. While they worked the women gossiped and laughed.

"What are you going to do?"

"I find Sister Serifina to tell her about the men. She must keep Lomida hidden." He disappeared as quietly as he had come.

"But, what did . . ." Maddie was talking to herself.

Quickly, she squeezed between two of the women, head down, and took up a half completed basket passed to her without a glance, and began to weave. No one even looked at her as the shouting men passed near. Maddie was glad that Diosune had shown her the basics of weaving along with teaching her about the different medicines and plants. It was another bond between the two women from such different ways of life. Although they had spent only a few days together, they had learned a lot from each other. Maddie fingered the strips of plant leaves, fighting to remain calm. To keep her mind off the dangerous men, she forced herself to recall where the basket colors came from—coreopsis made yellow and green dyes, yarrow was used for green and tan, and hollyhocks were used for a wide range of pink, blue and brown colors. Yucca plants were used for black, and bloodroot plants were good for red dye, but they grew in cooler areas so were used in the desert only when they were brought by traders. Maddie saw several deep red strips and realized that traders had been this way.

The women's fingers flew in and out of the reeds with a hypnotic effect. Some of the words Maddie understood, but the language was a mixture of Jumano-Apache and Spanish. She was comforted by her lack of identity. Each woman looked the same covered by faded shawls and long skirts. Maddie's blue skirt was dirty and indistinguishable from the others. Her shawl was as old as the others and hid her face as well. She was a white woman hiding in plain sight among women from the village, under the very noses of her pursuers. A faint smile raised the corners of her mouth at the irony of it all.

A commotion erupted in the courtyard as Luis and a glowering, angry Comes From War strode from the main church building. Father Lonigan followed behind them, gesturing and pointing right and left, still protesting the intrusion.

The bandits seemed to be talking at once and then threw open the chapel door and disappeared into the small chapel.

"Get out. Get out. We are in prayer 'ere!" An angry Sister Therese pushed the two protesting men backwards out of the chapel *"Vous n'avez aucune façon!* The sister was small but the men proved to be no match for the woman's fiery determination. The door closed in their faces and they were left looking at each other.

"Vamonos." Luis glanced at the women without actually seeing them, for he sought a white woman and a girl, and Maddie seemed no different from the others. Comes From War left Luis to watch the priest and went to the other side of the courtyard where he disappeared into the sisters' residence building. *Lomida's in there.* Maddie's heart sank with the certainty that they were about to be discovered.

A few minutes later Comes From War reappeared, crossed the courtyard and looked in the small infirmary. "They are not here!"

"Old man"—Luis turned to warn Father Lonigan— "if you hide them I will burn this place to the ground!" Luis and Comes From War went to their horses, mounted, and spurred them to a quick run and again jumped the low wall to ride back toward the village.

Where was Lomida? The chapel. Maddie was sure the girl was in there. She got up, hurried to the chapel door and cautiously opened it wide. Inside, four nuns, no, five nuns—one was much smaller than the others— knelt in prayer. Salvador sat in the corner on the back row, his hat in his hands. Maddie, looking askance, pointed to the smallest nun and Salvador nodded. Turning to leave, Maddie motioned for Salvador to follow her.

"Gracias, Salvador." She touched his cheek. "You saved us once again."

"Por nada, senorita." The boy swelled with embarrassed pride. "I did nothing."

Maddie took a breath. "Salvador. Now that we have a minute, when you went into Lajitas, what did you hear? Why are those men here?"

"The people say Chuy Ayala is calling for more men

to come here, many, many men. The *yanqui* soldiers from the fort are few, but brave, and they have a gun at Mesa de Anguila. I know the place they speak of. Apaches fight the whites and the black white men but could not take the gun. Chuy says the gun is his. He fought the Apaches who wanted the gun and made them run away. Soon he will go and take the gun from the soldiers. They are the same soldiers who came to get you and Miss Lomida, I think."

"Where is Luis going now?"

"He say they go to the cantina in town where Chuy's other men will come, and he will meet with Chuy." Salvador thought for a moment before continuing. "First they must drink their courage so it may be *manana* before they ride out."

Maddie said nothing. What to do? She had to get Lomida help and she needed to let the men from the fort know that she and Lomida were safe.

"Salvador. I have to go warn the soldiers. We can leave Lomida with the sisters but the men need to know that Chuy has many soldiers. I must tell them that we are safe for now but Lomida needs to get to Fort Davis so she can be taken care of as soon as possible."

"But, Miss Maddie . . ."

"Now, Salvador, tonight. You go get the horses ready, I'll go talk with Sister Serifina and tell Lomida goodbye and then we can go as soon as it's dark." She stopped, and then sighed in resignation. "I can't ask you to do this, Salvador. Your life will be at risk and here you are safe." What had she been thinking?

"I am your friend. I will do this." Salvador slipped away. Maddie wasted no time and headed back to the wing where Lomida was being kept. The girl was back in bed, a small litter placed against the wall revealed how the nuns had moved her so easily.

"Miss Maddie. Where have you been?" The girl was lying on a cot, and sat up as soon as she saw Maddie. "You'll never guess!"

"Why, Sister Lomida!"

"How did you know?" Lomida started to laugh and lifted the blanket. She still wore a black habit under the covers. "Isn't Sister Serifina smart?" Lomida started to cough, her weak body not able to keep up with the delight in tricking Luis and Comes From War.

Sister Serifina laughed with delight. "I did nothing. God played a little trick on those men. He made their eyes not see how small one of the sisters was." Sister Serifina went to Lomida and gave her some medicine to slow the cough. "They are not good men I think."

"Even so, Sister, I think you and the other sisters are wonderful people. You risk your lives for us." Maddie sat beside Lomida. "Now, Lomida, you must listen carefully to what I have to tell you." She then explained what she and Salvador were going to do.

"But, Miss Maddie, that's so dangerous. What if you get caught?"

"Salvador thinks the men will stay in town tonight and that will give us time to reach the soldiers before Chuy does. The men from Fort Davis need to know where we are." Maddie hesitated. "I don't know what else to do, Lomida. We put all of these people at risk if anything goes wrong."

Blue eyes peered over the covers, squeezed shut and

then reopened. "Okay. Do what you have to and be careful. I'll be fine. I promise." Once again the coughing took over and Lomida fell back in the bed.

Maddie hugged the little girl. "You are so brave, Lomida. Your father will be proud of you." She turned and hurried out the door before she broke down completely.

Chapter Twenty-nine

"**I** think if we try to ride out in the morning Leoni'll die," Butter said to Tilman. Having found cover behind some rocks, the men made some much-needed shade by using the tarp that had served as the Gatling's cover. "Them holes is crusted over, but when he moves they bust open again. He's plenty game to try, but I seen him a-lookin' under the dressing."

"We could tie him on his horse," Tilman said.

"Make no diff'rence," Butter said, "still kill 'im."

"Why don't the two of you ride," Burney interjected, surprising Tilman and Butter, who didn't know the officer was listening. "You go for help, and we'll hold out as long as we can." The young man's voice seemed to be recovering.

Trooper Lee had boiled some water and was washing Leoni's wounds. The holes were ragged, dark purple on the edges, but there were no signs of pus, and the wounds did not stink of corruption. Leoni's face and hands were deeply tanned by the sun, and the skin of his back and chest seemed unusually pale in comparison, making the wounds stand out even more. Before covering the wounds Lee dusted them liberally with crushed chaparral leaves the way Tilman had done.

"I'm holding you back. Why don't all of you ride?" Leoni offered. "Leave me a couple of carbines and pistols, and I'll hold them off while you get away."

"Man can't have no private conversation 'round here"—Butter laughed—"ever'body's gotta put in his two cents!"

"You soldiers must all want to be heroes," Tilman joked, recognizing the bravery of each man, "but you'll be dead ones for sure if we listen to you."

"Hey, I ain't ready to die just yet," Lee said. "I still got a couple of gals I want to see back in Baltimore."

"I got a Cherokee woman needs me over by Fort Griffin, and besides," Trooper Bell piped up from his firing position at the top of the knoll, pointing at Lee, "*he* owes me ten dollars so I gotta keep 'im alive at least till after next payday!"

"All right, let's hold for another day, and see how things look tomorrow."

"Mr. Burney, I suggest you set those Hotchkiss shells under the gun and the limber, and get the fuses ready to light," Tilman said, "so if things don't work out we can set 'em off."

"Sounds like a plan t'me!" Butter chuckled. "I'm hungry." And with that, Butter cut a thick slab of Army bacon, skewered it on a rifle cleaning rod, and set it to roasting over the coals of his coffee fire. "Where's that hard tack?"

* * *

The night was so dark Maddie could hardly see her horse's ears, much less the trail they followed. A thunderstorm far to the southwest sent occasional flashes of blue light across the land to provide glimpses of desolate hills. The wind brought distant thunder, adding to the tension Maddie felt.

Salvador spoke quietly, reassuringly, "The horses know all the trails here. Our horses come from *Senor* Goodnight when he drive cattle east of the Pecos River. They were night horses, but grew too old, too stiff to work the cattle, so he leave them for us. You have heard of him? No? Trust them to find good footing."

They rode through the night. Stiff and sore from her walk out of Santa Elena Canyon and the uphill grade following the bed of Terlingua Creek to Pepe's sheep camp, Maddie found that sitting astride the horse with only a sheep skin for a saddle created new aches. At least she was not on her feet, although she realized that where her bare legs under her skirt rubbed the horse's flanks, her skin was becoming irritated by the animal's sweat. *I'll have to collect more aloe,* Maddie thought. *How much further?* The horse's motion became monotonous, lulling her to sleep; Maddie's head sank to her chest and she nodded off.

The storm rained itself out somewhere far away, and the anvil-shaped clouds slowly dissipated, drifting south, no longer glowing inside by almost continuous lightning flashes. The wind stilled, and a pair of hunting owls called to each other as they flapped away from the intruding riders.

"There," Salvador whispered, reining his horse to a halt.

With a start Maddie jerked awake, blinking, rubbing her eyes as her horse stopped alongside Salvador's. In the near distance a small knoll appeared to rise from the desert blackness, visible because it seemed less dark than the backdrop of sky.

"We must be careful or they will shoot us," Salvador whispered.

"Stay here, I'll go," Maddie whispered. "Maybe they will know my voice."

Maddie slipped to the ground, wincing with stiffness. Salvador dismounted, took the reins of Maddie's horse, and squatted behind a rock to wait. Clumsily, Maddie made her way toward the knoll. The night grew colder.

Pebbles fell on Tilman. He awoke, listening, still, and easing out of his blanket, sat up. Sol Burney, sitting in the firing position on the crest of the knoll wrapped in his blanket against the cold, motioned for him to come near. After exhaling, Burney whispered, "Movement over there."

Tilman could see nothing. Stones clattered as someone lurched on a loose rock, followed by mumbled, indistinguishable words. What kind of bandit was this? An exasperated huff, and again mumbled words, "Where *are* they?"

Burney leaned close to Tilman saying, "That's a woman. And I think I know her!"

"What?" Tilman asked in a whisper, "Are you touched in the head?"

"No! I think that's the schoolteacher! I think that's Maddie Brown."

"Well, call out to her."

In a hoarse stage whisper, Burney called, "Miss Maddie?"

"Yes. *Yes!*" came a relieved reply. "It's me, so don't shoot. Please come and get me. I can't see."

"I'll go," Burney said.

Urgent words tumbled from Maddie as she explained about Chuy Ayala's men who would come with the morning light to kill them and take the gun. "Oh, Salvador's out there. I almost forgot. He brought me here and now he's out there waiting for me."

"Who?"

"Salvador. He's just a boy, but he helped save us."

"Well, don't call him in," Tilman said. "You go back to find him and ride away. You don't want to be here when the shooting starts. Stay with Lomida and we'll come and get you when we are done here."

"I'm staying."

"No, no you're not. This is no place for a woman or a boy."

"I'm not walking another step, mister whoever you are," Maddie replied indignantly. "I'm staying!"

"Tilman, I'm a-thinkin' this here's another one of them strong-willed women you always seem to run into," Butter said. "I believe this one means it."

"I do!" Maddie said.

"What kind of a lash-up is this?" Tilman said in exasperation. "All right, but don't bring that boy here. Call out and tell him to go home."

After a long pause, Maddie consented. Standing up, she asked, "Which way did I come from?"

"That way, Miss," Burney said. As he spoke, Butter motioned for them to look in the same direction.

"Miss Maddie. I believe we have found Salvador, or rather he has found us."

They all looked as Salvador came from the other side of the knoll, leading the horses.

"Some scouts we are. A young boy gets around us." Butter turned and went back to stand guard.

"Salvador, I'm safe." Maddie went to the young man. "Go back to the mission and tell Lomida what is going on and that we will be for her when we finish. If we don't return then you and the sisters need to get her to Fort Davis when you can."

Silence. Then Salvador nodded and, leading both horses, disappeared into the night as quietly as he had appeared.

"See to your guns, men," Burney said, "I've a feeling it's going to get hot out here when the sun comes up."

"Give me a rifle," Maddie demanded, "and show me where to go."

"A rifle?"

"I can shoot. The man I came to Texas to marry was a cavalryman, and he saw to it I knew how to shoot."

"What's the world coming to?" Tilman said.

"She can have my Winchester," Butter offered, "and I'll use one of them Springfields." Handing his rifle to Maddie, he continued, "Ain't you hungry, Miss? I can make us some coffee an' bacon."

Chapter Thirty

The cold dawn came in with the sun's pale yellow light filtering through a haze of low clouds far to the east. Breakfast—coffee, bacon and hard tack for those who wanted it—was over. Butter made sure the coffee pot sat in the coals of the fire. He might want some later. Nobody had much of an appetite, and nobody seemed to talk very much, either. In the hushed desert nothing moved, all life hunkered down and seemed to hold its breath anticipating violent death as if this was the start of the world's last day.

"There they are, Lieutenant!"

All eyes turned to the Mexican camp. Cheers and shouts and a few scattered pistol shots broke the desert silence. Burney trained his binoculars and studied the activity.

"Reinforcements. I can't be sure for all the dust and movement, but I think it's at least thirty men, maybe more." Turning to face his depleted command, Burney said, "Take your positions."

"Come alongside, Miss Maddie," Butter called, "you and me'll hold this side."

"Sergeant Leoni, use your pistols when they get close, and the rest of you, wait for my command."

"Just like the old days, right Butter?" Tilman reminisced.

"Riders coming!" Trooper Bell signaled, tossing his hat aside and taking up a prone firing position, his carbine held at the ready.

Two men rode out from the Mexican camp, one carrying a white flag. Preparations for battle continued behind them and a group of perhaps twenty riders circled around to the south toward the mesa, keeping well out of rifle range.

"Oye, gringos!" The riders halted about fifty yards from the knoll. Maddie recognized Luis, and with him, holding the white flag, was Comes From War. The Indian was mounted on a spirited paint horse that held his head high and danced nervously. Comes From War had painted his face a brilliant red from the mouth down, and above that a stark white so that he appeared even more fierce than before. She aimed her rifle at his chest, thumbed the hammer back and curled her finger around the trigger.

"Easy, missy," Butter whispered. "Wait for the lieutenant. You don't want to fire on a flag of truce." When Maddie turned her face to Butter he was surprised at the cold anger in her eyes. "Friend of yours, I reckon?"

"I hear you," Burney answered Luis, pulling himself up to a kneeling position. His strong voice had returned.

"You give us the gun; we let you go in peace. We all go home an' celebrate Christmas, eh?"

"We'll keep the gun, and we'll let *you* go in peace," Burney shouted.

"No. I don' think so." Luis was quiet for a moment. "Listen, *gringo,* I offer you your lives. Give us the gun."

"Okay, but here are our terms," Burney said calmly, "we'll give you the gun . . ."—he smiled—"one bullet at a time."

Comes From War's searching eyes found Maddie's. With a malicious smile he spoke to Luis.

"Come, my sweet," Luis called, "you do not wish to die here with these crazy men."

Maddie's blunt reply startled Tilman and Burney, and brought a laugh from Butter and Leoni. Bell and Lee howled with glee.

Angered, Luis and Comes From War wheeled their horses and whipped them into a run back to their camp.

"Sorry, it just came out," Maddie said shyly.

Burney watched as men formed a skirmish line and stepped out from the Mexican camp. Each kept about ten yards distance from the next man, while all were carrying their rifles at the ready across their chests, like bird hunters. No bunching up to offer easy targets, they moved from cover to cover in quick dashes. It was clear that the men he faced today had at least some military training and would not be easily beaten.

To the south, the single file of riders slowed, on command turned by the left flank to face the knoll, and halted about eight hundred yards away. Chuy's plan became obvious. He intended to send skirmishers forward, get them fairly close and take the knoll under fire to keep the Americans pinned down. Then the mounted men would gallop across the plain. At the last minute when the riders were almost to the knoll the foot soldiers would cease firing and begin their own charge at the knoll. By using their momentum, the mounted men planned to overrun and wipe out the defenders on the knoll. A few minutes only were needed, and then it would all be over. Tilman had to admire the thinking behind the plan.

Wasting few words, Burney told everyone what to expect. "At West Point we studied the history of war. Men say brave things in times like these. At a place called Bunker Hill, during the American Revolution, Colonel William Prescott was outnumbered by the British and had very little ammunition. He told his colonials 'no firing till you see the whites of their eyes.' When they come for us now, let 'em get close and make every shot count!"

As if to punctuate his remarks, the first scattered shots came from the skirmishers to their front.

"Here they come!"

The fire, not returned from the knoll, soon mounted in intensity. The skirmishers became bolder, standing longer between shots. They were now barely three hundred yards from the knoll.

"Pick your targets," Tilman said calmly.

Burney raised his hand, paused and then dropped it, shouting "Fire! Commence firing!"

At the first volley five skirmishers tumbled to the ground. Only one regained his feet, hobbling to the rear, dragging one leg.

"Wagner, take those riders under fire with your Winchester!"

The riders were still holding, waiting for the skirmishers to get closer to the knoll. Tilman quickly shifted his position, thumbed up the peep sight, set it for six hundred yards, and with his first shot killed one of the horses, trapping its rider underneath when it reared and fell. As fast as he could work the lever action, Tilman continued to fire into the riders and emptied one saddle. "There's a feller won't need that hoss anymore!" Tilman shouted above the noise. When the man was knocked from his horse, the horses on either side panicked at the smell of blood and began pitching and bucking, throwing one of the surprised riders to the ground. When the other horse ran away his unfortunate rider, ineffectually hauling back on the reins, found himself carried directly to the knoll. As he approached, Leoni said, "He's mine," and calmly leveled his pistol. At twenty-five yards he fired and the riderless horse passed by at a dead run, empty stirrups flapping.

The skirmishers went to ground and continued to advance by crawling from cover to cover, firing, moving, and firing. Tilman reloaded, and then began to fire more carefully into the riders.

A cry of pain came from Butter, and he and Maddie stopped firing. Butter cussed, and hollered for another rifle. "What's doing, old man?" Tilman shouted.

"Feller hit the action of my rifle!"

"They shot his finger off!" Maddie yelled, grabbing hold of his hand. "Will you be still?"

"I tell you it ain't nothin'."

"Don't you die!"

"I ain't a-gonna die!"

"Be still and let me fix it."

Tilman resumed firing. Let Butter and Maddie fight it out.

"They got Bell!"

"Keep firing!"

A bullet smacked into the rock Lee hid behind for cover and sprayed jagged fragments of rock into his face and scalp. He was having trouble seeing from all the blood running into his eyes, and struggled to wrap his kerchief around his head to slow the bleeding from the scalp wounds. Worse, he'd stopped firing, and men advanced still closer, redoubling their fire against the weakening *norteamericanos*. Reloading again, Tilman burned his hand on the smoking hot barrel of his rifle, but continued to shove the shells into the loading port as fast as he could. Suddenly, with a sound like thunder the wave of riders came whipping and spurring at the knoll. It would soon be over. Tilman dropped the rifle and palmed his .45, ready for close work. He watched as the distance grew shorter and shorter. The riders began firing, but too soon, and they weren't hitting anybody; few men are accurate when shooting from horseback at a target beyond point-blank range.

An ear-splitting whistling shriek followed immediately by a flash and a deafening explosion burst flame and white smoke in the center of the line of horsemen. Another shriek ending in another explosion among the on-rushing riders, this one head-high, sprayed deadly shrapnel into man and horse, knocking them sprawling. The line broke in pandemonium, riders turning and racing hard to the south and the border, racing to be anywhere away from the awful sudden whistling death. Now came the sharp report from the north.

"Artillery!" shouted Burney, "they brought the howitzers!"

At the same moment a bugle sounded "Charge."

Tilman, Maddie and Burney stood for a better look, while Butter waved a bandaged hand and they all cheered as a line of cavalry troopers led by Lieutenant Dielmann Zook thundered past the knoll. Zook stood in his stirrups and leaned forward screaming his battle cry with his outstretched sabre flashing in the sun. Hard-eyed, blue-uniformed Buffalo Soldiers began firing as they closed on the laggard bandits.

Rifle and pistol fire they could stand, but Chuy's men were not prepared to endure shelling from a Hotchkiss mountain howitzer, nor could they face the battle-seasoned troopers of the 10th U.S. Cavalry. With Chuy and Luis leading the panicked retreat far to the rear, El Chamuscado's fighters quickly and wisely chose discretion as the better part of valor and, continuing their run for the border, opted to fight another day.

From his position in the distant rocks, Agapito, the long shooter, gathered his few belongings. He would join Chuy across the river.

Maddie searched for and finally saw Comes From War's paint horse, now riderless, running away with the other horses.

From the artillery position four riders galloped out, one carrying a red and white swallowtail pennant, and rode to the knoll, horses sliding to a halt, dancing, nervous with eyes flashing white from the excitement of battle.

"Good morning, sir"—Burney snapped off a crisp West Point salute to Captain Law and grinned—"I sure am glad to see you."

"Sorry I'm late, Lieutenant, but the howitzer slowed our march," Law answered. "At least we got in on some of the fun. I see you've got some wounded. We'll see to them and I'll take your report directly." Turning to his runner, Law said, "Bring up the surgeon!" and the man wheeled and rode for the ambulances now trundling toward the knoll. "First Sergeant, set up a command post . . ."—Law looked around and selected a nearby terrace of level ground—"over there and have Mr. Zook report to me. Bugler, sound 'Recall.'"

John Law dismounted and shook hands with Tilman. "I was never so glad to see Yankee artillery in my life," Tilman said. "John, you saved us today."

Butter, holding up a bandaged right hand to stop the bleeding, offered his left to Law. "About time y' all got here, we're almost out of coffee," Butter said.

Touching a hand to the brim of his hat Law said to Maddie, "Miss Brown, I'm glad to see you safe, but where's Lomida?"

"She's fine, John." In her excitement, Maddie forgot to call him Captain Law as she usually did. "Lomida is at the mission by Lajitas. It's only a short ride from here. Salvador, the boy who brought me here, has probably returned to tell them what's happening. Lomida has been ill but the sisters at the mission are taking care of her and she's much better." Maddie paused to catch her breath. "I'd like to be there when she sees you."

John looked at Burney. "Lieutenant, take care of the wounded and reform the troop. Sweep the field and see that the dead are buried. Do you think you can head this patrol back to Fort Davis if I go get my daughter?"

"Yes, sir!"

"Do so. We'll catch up to you on the trail."

Burney immediately left to carry out his new orders.

"Tilman. Let's go get my daughter and visit the mission. I might like to stop and say a prayer of thanksgiving myself." He turned to Maddie. "Miss Brown, if you will lead the way."

Chapter Thirty-one

"It's Tennessee sour mash," John said as he opened the bottom drawer on his desk. He withdrew a bottle and, breaking the seal, poured dark amber liquid into two glasses. "The last of the post-action reports are done, the colonel has signed off on them, and they're ready for mailing to headquarters in San Antonio. I've been saving this for a special occasion and I deem today is the day."

Raising his glass in salute, John offered a toast. "As my first sergeant always says, 'May you be one hour in heaven before the Devil knows you're dead!" John drained his glass and slammed the empty on his desk. "Not as good as Uncle Charl' used to make, but it'll do."

Tilman barely sipped the whiskey, held his glass, and sat quietly.

"What's wrong, Tilman?"

"I've been thinking. It's odd that Colonel Grierson happened to return early from New Mexico and sent you after us, made you bring that mountain howitzer along, and then you just happened to be on that ridge when those people got ready to attack us. Without all those just happened tos we'd never have got off that hill alive."

"And we might not have found Lomida at the mission," John said. "What's your point?"

"Well, I wonder why all those things happened that way. Was it only coincidence?"

"Nothing happens by coincidence, Tilman."

"That's what Sarah used to say."

John poured himself a short drink, tossed it off. With a glance at the wall clock, John said, "I've got to make my rounds of the post. Show the flag, you might say. Come along, the fresh air will do you some good."

The door closed and for the first time in weeks Maddie stopped. After a few days in the post hospital for observation—Susannah and Surgeon Phillips had insisted—she was finally back in the small room that she called home. Safely back at last, she paused to remember the reception they had received. Imagine, even Nettie Wordsmith seemed glad to see her. She looked around her room. Apparently someone had come in and kept it dusted. Fresh roses from the Phillips' garden graced the top of her dresser.

Her room had a different look. Why? The bed. On her bed was a beautiful Lone Star quilt. She knew without looking that it was made by the women of the fort. Sudden tears spilled down her face. She didn't know why they had done this but it was the prettiest thing she had ever owned. The quilt was a cream with the star done in reds and blues. She knew she would cherish it forever. An envelope lay on her pillow.

Maddie sat in the rocker by the pot-bellied stove and opened the note.

This is a token of our esteem and affection, Maddie. You did what few of us could have done. We are glad to have you back and would love for you to join us next Tuesday evening at seven pm at my house for our quilting club. Indeed, we would be honored.

We hope you enjoy this quilt as much as we enjoyed making it. Many of these stitches are over-laid with the prayers we said for your and Lomida's safe return.

Susannah Phillips

Carefully closing the note and slipping it back in the envelope, Maddie placed the letter in a small chest under her bed. As she stood, a prickle of fear raised the small hairs on the back of her neck. Something was different. What had changed? A shadow from the lamp where no shadow had been! Quickly she turned and was face to face with . . . Comes From War.

He was dirty and one arm was wrapped with a rag. Crusted blood stained his head scarf. His eyes glittered with hate. The black of the darkest night was light compared to the anger in his brutal face.

"You mine!" he hissed. "I come for you and now we go."

Before Maddie was able to draw a breath to scream, Comes From War clamped his dirty hand over her mouth, drew her body forcefully against his own. She could smell the dirt, the sweat and the stench of battle on him.

"Mmmmff!" Quickly Maddie's mouth was covered

with a rag and she grimaced as Comes From War spun her around and twisted the cloth to tie it at the back of her head, catching pieces of her hair with it as he made the knot.

"You be my woman." He pushed Maddie toward the door. "You learn to obey."

Maddie tried to think of what to do, how to resist, but she couldn't scream and was overpowered. The schoolhouse had been built on the edge of the parade ground and there were no soldiers' quarters by the school. Besides, it was evening and most soldiers would be in their barracks by now. What was she to do? Comes From War pushed her to the door and her knees gave way from fear. As she fell Maddie jerked one hand from his grasp and in desperation reached for the linen cloth on her dresser. If she could reach the heavy glass vase maybe she could strike him with it and escape! She tugged the linen but the glass vase of roses fell to the flagstone floor and shattered, the breaking glass loud in the silence of her room. Several books also fell with a resounding thump.

Comes From War pulled her up from the floor. "Stop. No more!" A short rope soon held her arms behind her as she tried to twist her hands loose. Once her hands were bound struggle would be futile, escape impossible. Maddie moaned in rage and frustration.

Over the sound of her own labored breathing she thought she heard the sound of footsteps. It was her imagination. Maddie had been so close. She tried not to cry as Comes From War pushed her through the doorway onto the steps. As Maddie stepped out, she was suddenly thrust aside by an unknown arm and saw a blue uniform as John Law, gun in hand, brushed past her colliding with Comes From War, the two men thumping to the floor of her room. Tilman Wagner made sure Maddie was out of harm's way.

Terrible sounds came from the room, animal-like grunts of a life or death struggle, things being knocked to the floor, fists thudding into flesh, a yelp of pain and something metallic clattered across the stones, then Comes From War burst past Maddie and Tilman followed by John. They disappeared around the schoolhouse and then there were two shots and silence.

Tilman cut the rope that held Maddie's hands and with quaking hands she quickly removed the filthy rag from her mouth. "Are you okay, Miss Maddie?"

John came around the corner, his gun back in his holster. He motioned to Tilman who excused himself as several curious neighbors came out to see what the ruckus was about. Maddie rushed to John and fell into his arms. A surprised John hesitated, then put his arms around the frightened woman and held her tightly as she tried to hold back her tears.

The sergeant of the guard came running with a shouted, "Captain! What's all the shootin' about?" He stopped short, surprised to see the officer embracing the schoolteacher.

"Are you all right, Miss Brown?" John asked.

"I'll be fine. You saved my life"—she shuddered— "again. What about Comes From War?"

"He won't bother you again. You can rest assured of that."

"I'm grateful." Maddie gasped for something to say. "I thought I heard something but really didn't expect . . ."

"Tilman and I happened to be making my rounds before calling it a night. We thought we had everything taken care of, but maybe we spoke too soon."

"It doesn't matter. You were here. That's what counts." Maddie stopped, awkward, not sure what to say. Neither wanted to let go of the other. *Say something, say anything, you ninny.* "Lomida?"

"She is fine. Last I looked, Annie and Lomida were discussing everything in detail." He paused. "I will never be able to repay you."

"Captain Law. You just repaid me if there was any repaying to do. We're even, okay?" She dropped her arms, regaining her composure. John released her. She smiled sadly. As far as John Law was concerned she was Lomida's teacher. That was all.

"Well, I tell you what then, Madeline Brown. If we're even then perhaps you'll help me out. I need a partner for the regiment's homecoming ball on Saturday night. Will you do me the honor?"

"I don't know, John, I . . ." She started to turn back to her room, afraid to show the confusion she felt.

"I want to get to know you better, Madeline. Not because of Lomida, mind you, even though I know she thinks you are wonderful. Wait!" John placed his hands on Maddie's shoulders and turned her to face him. "Don't run off. I'm not through. I realized while you were gone with Lomida that I worried about you as well, more than I had imagined possible." He continued as Maddie tried to keep her mouth closed. "So what do you say?"

All she could do was nod in speechless agreement.

John chuckled, "Don't worry. You are no more surprised at me than I am."

Several of the wives arrived and protectively gathered up Maddie and ushered her into her room. John and Tilman watched as the door closed. They turned and John said, "Shall we continue our rounds?"

Chapter Thirty-two

Knocking, followed by pounding, followed by "May I come in and look?" and a creaking door hinge told Maddie that Lomida was not waiting for an answer.

"Come on in. I need help anyway." Maddie was busy arranging a troublesome bustle. She didn't realize that Lomida wasn't alone until she turned at the sound of a man clearing his throat.

"Oh, John, I didn't see you." Maddie blushed as red as the flowers that the good captain had in his hand. "Where did you get those beautiful flowers?" They both laughed as they simultaneously said "the Phillips' garden, where else!"

Lomida danced excitedly around the room, the uneven growth of her legs manifested in an increasingly awkward rolling gait. "Oh, I just love dances. Don't you, Miss Maddie?" She caught Maddie in a hug, pulling her around with her. "Oh, I forgot. Your bustle."

Both of them started giggling as they looked at the

precariously hung, dark green satin material gathered in a bow that listed to the side of Maddie's new dress.

"Here. Let me help." Lomida turned Maddie around and efficiently hooked the bustle to where it rode right in the middle of Maddie's lower back, just the way it should. "Your dress is beautiful. Did you make this yourself?"

"No, Lomida. Fortunately for me, Susannah came over last week and offered to help me make this in time for the dance. Nettie Wordsmith even brought over the satin for the bustle." She turned to John. "You didn't have anything to do with that now, did you?"

"No, I didn't. Although I am glad to see the ladies have realized that you are not the vixen they wanted to think you were." John admired the way that Maddie had recovered her composure in the week since the incident with Comes From War. She had reopened school, kept an eye on Lomida as she recovered, and had graciously accepted the belated amends of the officers' wives. "I must say you look lovely, Madeline." He saw Lomida watching him closely. "As do you, Lomida."

"Annie helped me with my dress." Lomida turned slowly and the ice-blue taffeta of her simple dress accentuated her dark red hair. "She is very upset still about her brother. I told her that was silly. We can't help our family." She looked to Maddie as if to confirm this wisdom she had heard from someplace. "Isn't that what you always say, Poppa?"

John helped Maddie with her wrap. She was excited about the dance, but anxious as well. On the captain's arm she knew that she would turn a few eyes but she was pleased to be going with him and with Lomida as well. She could handle the others. "Ready, Captain Law?" She smiled up at John as she placed her hand on his sleeve. "I might add, that you look most handsome in that fancy dress uniform yourself. Doesn't he, Lomida?"

John was wearing his best dark-blue wool that was lined with black polished cotton. The double-breasted coat with three button cuffs had fourteen brightly polished brass buttons. "Thanks, Madeline. I have to admit I am vain enough to miss the gold lace that was on the older sleeves, but this new style is easier to keep. Although," he continued as they went out the door, "it is still mighty hot, even for December."

"Well, it does look nice, doesn't it, Lomida?" Maddie and Lomida, on each side of John, walked the short distance to the commissary warehouse, the only place large enough on the post for a dance.

"My but it is beautiful." Pungent juniper boughs along with big clumps of mistletoe were strategically placed about the ceiling of the building. Regimental colors, national colors and troop pennants flanked the bandstand. Multi-colored popcorn balls and chains of colored paper were draped around the room to add to the festive look. Red and pink blooms of Christmas cacti decorated tables that were heaped with roast turkey, venison, beef and mutton, pickles, and a variety of canned vegetables. There were mincemeat pies and fruitcakes made by the officers' ladies, and Annie's pumpkin empanadas. There were even oysters on ice, ordered months ago and imported especially for the occasion by Colonel Grierson. An enormous gingerbread house was the centerpiece.

"Oh, look, Miss Maddie." Lomida longingly eyed the gingerbread house. "Isn't it wonderful!"

Maddie agreed. The building had been transformed. She nodded to Tilman and Butter as she saw them standing at the opposite end of the table. Butter was deep in conversation with Neala Barry, the baker from the town that abutted the fort. Watching Neala with Butter, even though she stood a head taller than he, Maddie couldn't help but notice that the two were having quite a conversation and neither seemed eager to quit talking.

"Are you seeing what I see?" Susannah had quietly come up by Maddie's side. She smiled as she indicated Butter and Neala.

"Well, that would take the cake!" Maddie smiled mischievously at her unintended pun.

Susannah laughed. "You look lovely, Maddie. That green is definitely your color and I am so pleased to see you here with the captain tonight." With that blessing, Susannah disappeared to welcome someone else as the evening continued.

Eating gave way to the regimental band's smaller dance group and everybody applauded, ready for the music. Colonel Grierson formally opened the ball by asking the regimental Sergeant Major O'Rourke's wife Mary for the first dance while the sergeant major asked Alice Grierson. As they danced the first waltz others joined them, boots and dress shoes shuffling on the wood floor sprinkled earlier with sawdust so movement would be easier. Butter and Neala circled the floor several times causing several comments. Madeline and John danced and then Tilman asked if Madeline would dance and they began a waltz. Looking past Tilman's shoulder Madeline was secretly pleased that she had spoken with Mr. Zook soon after arriving at the dance. She watched as the dashing Lieutenant Zook, under arms with his saber and spurs and kepi as required of the post's officer of the day, saluted and formally asked John's permission and then took the floor to dance with a blushing Lomida.

After the band paused for its first break, Colonel Grierson made a few remarks about the joyous season made happier by the regiment's limited but successful actions against Victorio. He acknowledged the escape by Lomida and Maddie from Chuy Ayala's camp and praised them for their courage and endurance. He recounted Burney's and Law's decisive action with the raiders, and announced that Law, Burney and Zook had been mentioned in dispatches for their boldness and initiative and in conclusion said he would not be surprised if Law were to be brevetted a major in the coming year. Glasses were charged and the regimental toast was given, "Long live the United States and success to the regiment!"

The band took its place and resumed with lively polkas, Alice Grierson's favorite dance, and more waltzes and schottisches.

"A lovely evening, Miss Maddie. Wouldn't you say?" Tilman smoothly moved her over the floor trying to remember the last time he danced a waltz.

"Oh, I agree, Tilman. Are you planning to stay long here? I couldn't help but notice that you seem a little melancholy."

"You know what, Miss Maddie? You are right. I miss Catherine, the lady I left in Colorado. We only realized that we cared for each other when I came to help John, but now that you and Lomida are at home and safe I think it's time for me to get back to Colorado." He smiled for the first time. "In fact, if I excuse myself now I can get ready to go and leave on the westbound stage that pulls out first thing in the morning."

Butter and Neala waltzed by, his head reaching her shoulder as they sashayed by. "Looks like I may be traveling back alone though. I will miss Butter, for I've grown used to having his company. No man could ask for a truer friend, but it looks like he is going to be occupied here for a while."

Tilman stopped by the door and turned to Maddie. "Do me a favor. I don't like good-byes. Never have. Tell John for me that he knows where I will be. I'll talk to Butter after the dance." Tilman bowed, got his hat from the table and turned back to Maddie as he started out the door. "Tell John that for the first time in years, I am eager to go home."

Afterword

Tilman had arrived back at Catherine's ranch the day before Christmas and had amazed everyone, including himself by kneeling and proposing when Catherine answered his knock at her front door. Paul Fry, the itinerant minister, had been over for supper as usual and had burst out laughing.

"Tilman Wagner. Don't you take the cake? Meet this woman, woo her for a short time, run off to Texas to save some people, and then show up here and fall on your knees."

"Paul Fry! You should be ashamed of yourself." Catherine blushed, traced Tilman's dear face with her hands to assure herself he was fine. "The answer, by the way, is yes indeed I will marry you."

"Wow. What a way to start the new year!" James was beside himself. He had no memory of the father who had died when he was young but Tilman had captured the boy's heart when he treated him like the man of the family and taught him to conquer his fear of being one

209

of the smallest boys in his class. "Will I be a Wagner too?" He held his breath as he waited for an answer.

"If your mother says that is okay, we will ride over to the courthouse and have a lawyer draw up the papers as soon as possible." Tilman was very fond of the boy and he intended to be a much better father this time.

Pastor Fry married Catherine and Tilman on New Year's Day and 1880 was proving to be a wonderful year already. Tilman and Catherine were working hard, happier than either of them knew was possible, striving to make their new marriage work. The day before school got out for the summer Tilman shared a letter with Catherine he received from his friend John.

Tilman,

Once again I want to congratulate you on your new marriage. I hope to meet Catherine and James when I can. Lomida is doing wonderfully. The new surgeon in El Paso graciously consented to come here for a consultation and after operating on her leg it is straighter and will make walking easier for her. She will always limp and will need special shoes, but she already has much less pain.

Butter is doing fine. He is courting Neala, the baker. I think Butter has proven the old saying that the way to a man's heart is through his stomach. Neala is quite a woman. She stands about 6 inches taller than Butter and is probably skinny as she is tall. They are quite the talk of the post.

While we are at it I should tell you that Madeline Brown and I are also seeing each other. She has spent many hours over here with Lomida trying to keep her caught up with her schoolwork and Sergeant-Major (yes, Sheridan promoted him) Leoni's wife always accompanies her so the post's ladies know all is well.

Leoni's wound has almost completely healed from the inside with no hint of gangrene. Surgeon Phillips is studying the use of chaparral on such cases and is following the work along the same lines by a man called Lister, thanks to you.

Madeline is a fine young woman. I was worried about her being ten years younger than me but she doesn't seem to care and I think by the time you get this letter I will probably have got up my nerve and proposed to her. I think Madeline, Lomida, and I will make a fine team.

Once again I want to thank you for always being my friend and helping me in time of need.
Sincerely,
John Law
Brevet Major, 10th U.S. Cav

Tilman sat with the letter in his hand. "What do you think of that, Catherine?"

"I think it is wonderful. Is Butter serious? I really miss him but I know he would love a family of his own. Except for old Sheriff he has always been alone." Catherine and Tilman sat on the porch, the early summer evening starting to cool down quickly as the sun went behind the Sawatch Mountains.

"Excuse me. Is anybody listening?" James sat impatiently, his leg jiggling as he tried to stay quiet.

"I'm sorry, James." Catherine smiled and reached down to tussle James' unruly hair. His red locks went every which way and there were pieces of hay mixed in his hair. "Where have you been?"

"That's what I'm trying to tell you, Mom." Grabbing his mother's hand he pulled her up and led her off the porch. He winked conspiratorially at Tilman as he led Catherine into the barn and to the last stall on the other side of Needles, Tilman's horse. A small dun-colored horse, barely fourteen hands high, stretched his head out over the gate for Catherine to scratch, a white star between black eyes. James looked expectantly at Catherine. "I'll take care of him. I promise."

"Old Sheriff, down at the stables in Buena Vista, told me last week that Ned Rhinehart out on the Rafter R had a cutting horse to sell. He won't be real big but he is a good sure-footed cow pony and will do for James to learn to ride. So, if you don't object. . . ." Tilman looked at Catherine, as eager as James. "I already bought him all the tack he'll need."

"Well. I know when I'm outnumbered. If your father says it is okay"—Catherine smiled—"then I think it is good for you to have your own horse."

"Oh, thanks, Mom and Dad. I'll name him Star, I think. Because of his face, you know." James promptly forgot the adults as he poured a bait of corn into the manger for the first horse he ever owned. Tilman and Catherine, holding hands, headed back for the house.

Pastor Fry rode up just as they reached the house. He drew up on his mount and smiled. "You two look like a couple of young'uns." He laughed while he dismounted. "Good to be back for a while. I have news for you, but let me stable my horse."

Sitting at the table with coffee, Paul Fry reached into his coat pocket. "Here, Catherine. This is for you. If it had been addressed to Tilman I think I might have lost it on the way out here." He handed her a yellow envelope. "Picked it up on my way from Buena Vista."

Catherine opened the envelope. "It's from my brother in New Mexico. It's not like him to send a telegram." Catherine frowned. "Excuse me." She went out on the porch and sat down in the swing.

American Rapid Telegraph
Company of Colorado
Telegram
June 12, 1880
Catherine Wagner
Buena Vista, Colorado

Urgent. Need help. Please come. David

Tilman came out onto the porch. One look at Catherine's troubled face was enough. "Well, bad news won't get any better if you keep it to yourself. What is it?" She handed Tilman the telegram and waited while he read it.

"How can we just leave everything, Tilman, to go to David? We have cattle and the garden is planted and . . . ?"

Paul stood at the screen door, looking out at them both. "I don't know the problem, but if you have to go away for a while, I may be able to help. I went to town today because the mayor and the town council have voted to give us a couple of town lots for a community church and they want me to head it up. That means I'll be here for good now, not traveling all over the dang country like before." He stopped, trying to gauge their reaction. "I need a place to stay and I could use the side yard for services for a while till we get up a building. It will take time but for now we can set up benches under the trees. Remember, I grew up on a farm so I can handle everything. Besides, we can always use the barn if it rains. What do you think?"

Catherine and Tilman looked at each other knowing that an answer had been provided and they must go. Tilman turned to Paul. "If you'll manage here, then Catherine, James and I can go help David. I need to meet the rest of my new family anyway. Right, Catherine?"

"You don't mind, Tilman? I know this isn't what you bargained for . . ." Catherine looked at her new husband, loving him even more for not questioning her brother or his request.

Tilman took Catherine's hand. "You are something else, Catherine Wagner. Yes you are. I am a lucky man." He paused. "I hear it's mighty warm in New Mexico in the summer. We best leave our winter things here with the parson." They all went inside the house, excitement entering as well. The next adventure loomed on the new horizon.